The Old Gents

Jose Yglesias

Arte Público Press
Houston, Texas
1996

This volume is made possible through grants from the National Endowment for the Arts (a federal agency), the Andrew W. Mellon Foundation and the Lila Wallace-Reader's Digest Fund.

Recovering the past, creating the future

Arte Público Press
University of Houston
Houston, Texas 77204-2090

Cover illustration and design by James F. Brisson

Yglesias, Jose
The old gents / by Jose Yglesias.
p. cm.
ISBN 1-55885-161-5 (cloth)
I. Title.
PS3575.G5O4 1996
813'.54—dc20 96-13274
CIP

The paper used in this publication meets the requirements of the American National Standard for Permanence of Paper for Printed Library Materials Z39.48-1984. ♾

Contents

The Old Gents

If you don't love me, love whom you please,
But throw your arms round me, give my heart ease.
    Give your heart ease, dear, give my heart ease.
    Throw your arms round me, give my heart ease.

Down In the Valley

For Death is a simple thing,
    And he go from door to door,
And he knock down some, and he cripple up some,
    And he leave some here to pray.

Lord, Remember Me!

Love

If I get too fancy, skip a couple of sentences. I always come down to earth. People see in me this old New York gent and they ask me directions and continue on (once I've answered in detail and with pleasure: I love this city) saying to themselves how right they had been, these violent days, to stop a nice old man, a regular person, and not one of the questionable characters in the Village. Greenwich Village, that is. So many look spaced out, so many dressed to shock. And it is true I am a regular down-to-earth person: I always know how much is in my savings account. But I am also an unknown quantity apt to go off on tangents and up into the stratosphere of fantasy. Even in these last sobering moments of my life. This is what this story is about—and come what may I shall tell a story. That's my pact with the reader.

In fact, to have chosen to live in the Village is something no one in Tampa (my hometown) could have appreciated. I live here because of a youthful fancy about myself, a flight into my sort of reality. When I was fifteen I read about the Provincetown Playhouse in a magazine at the Public Library in downtown Tampa (I used to rollerskate the many blocks from the Latino section of the city) and so I went looking for the Village when I got to New York in the late thirties.

I belonged there, that's what I thought, I was an artist—ha-ha!—from reading one magazine article and looking at a photograph of Edna St. Vincent Millay. Actually, I meant a writer, but saying an artist then allowed you more leeway: it was more a state of mind than anything specific. You didn't need an easel and paints and brushes to qualify, or a Leica or even a typewriter. And that's how my life took off—moseying around the Village—and is now ending. (I *am* a writer; you can look me up in *Who's Who*.) A youthful ploy; indeed, a purposeful misreading. I like to think about it that way. Don't you also pinpoint the happening that led to your life?

I like the young man I was then. The late thirties and the war, what a time! The old person I am now is someone who is being put to the test. A sobering time, I say, but I refuse to be glum about it. I was content with that Old Gent, as I call myself, until I went to the doctor three months ago. What shall I make of the Old Gent in the days to come? A new persona for my death sentence. If you cannot plan a flight of fancy, you can, perhaps, waylay it. I'm gonna try. As the young heroes of the sentimental stuff of my youth—an Odets play, a Steinbeck novel—might say, Come on, life, come on.

I do not have a magazine article as my guide, as did that boy with a perpetual hard-on in the late thirties. But I am beseeched to fashion a new life by that killer of old men: prostate cancer. By which I mean that I am thinking keenly about alternatives as I go about my life, what is left of it. My darling Gwendolyn, when she moved into the apartment down the hall six months ago and in time lifted me up and lit me up, did not, at first, shake me up as much, but cancer is thought to be more unsettling than love. How should I live my days now? Oh, you could sing that if you had an air. My cardiologist (yes, there are many things wrong with me) sent me to a urologist and he ordered tests at a couple of other offices after he had himself poked around in that nether region James Joyce first lifted to the level of consciousness among literary folk. Cloacal was a trendy adjective once. Twenty years ago, the urologist, Alec Hamilton, might have dissimulated, told my nearest relative first and then...I won't pursue this, that way lies fiction.

I don't write anymore, but I keep a journal. No, nothing that formal, nothing literary either; a diary is more like it. I had better quote from the diary the day he used a greased probe: *For sonogram I wore paper robe open at back, lay on side, looked at wall not him (he is descended from the colonial Hamilton and must feel he owns New York) and tried not to think of female nurse also in room. Biopsy snips made me wince. Didn't take long, then sat in his office, listened to him and came home. Sure I have cancer. I am to call him tomorrow.*

Something wrong with that diary entry. Inelegant. Not art. The writing, that is; or at least not artful. In fact, that was not the last sentence in the diary for the day; I gave the score of the Mets-Padres game I watched and listed the phone calls I received, including a sales pitch from MCI. The diary is merely useful, that's all. Definitely not literature. I am reminded of my friend Feltscher the sculptor. (In New York City, Jewish locutions take over your speech.) We had, because of the women we were then married to, been in and out of a couple of kitschy shops in Bar Harbor that day. He was irascible, he always was. "You don't seem to like folk art," I said. He took time to scowl before he replied, then said, "It's not art, that's why!" That's the trouble with diaries, too. They can provide clues, but they don't tell you what the day was really like, as does my own memory of that unair-conditioned summer day in Maine—or as would a fiction I could manipulate into being.

Is this the proper setting to speak eloquently about what informs art? A disquisition, while I lie on my side and look at the wall, like Proust's narrator during the last section of that portmanteau of a novel. *He* is about to enter the ballroom of the new Princesse des Guermantes, in fact that old shit Madame de Verdurin... Things are not what they seem, get it? Mine would have the advantage of a homey setting—well, not exactly homey, a urologist's office while accommodating a probe up my ass, but certainly down to earth—and a more active narrative to follow. (Promises, promises.) Proust's story and setting are irremediably glamorous: a hero who suffers some sort of spiritual malaise stepping into a major society event of the Paris season, and it is no wonder his view of what art is and his practice of it lie out of hand's reach. Not mine—ha-ha! Art must keep you on the edge of your seat, but in Proust there are too many moments when you do so because you want to spring out of it and see what's in the refrigerator.

But enough of that, or the reviewers will be right about my still being struck in my generation's modernist mode—should I turn this outpouring into a novel. Should I? What's the plot? I am dying. I am in love with Gwendolyn and she is twenty-four. She lives down the hall in another one-bedroom with her two-year-old boy Owen, and she keeps declaring her love for me whenever I pause between sentences. There are two young men in her life: her husband or, in any case, Owen's father; and a likeable young fellow across the hall from her and around the corner from me who seems to be going in and out of her apartment at all hours. Why do I say "seems?"—I know. His name is Thom. I nodded to him in the elevator once or twice before my darling Gwendolyn moved in, but I knew nothing about him, not even his name, until a few days before Gwendolyn left for L.A. He has taken to calling me Dad. I did not know them well before the L.A. venture, and certainly the situation was not as complicated as now, although I knew I was in love, ah yes.

Yes, I think there's a story in all this.

I am, indeed, a Dad. I have three sons. Randy, three blocks away (he is as important to this story as anyone), busy as hell writing screenplays and overseeing New York University's film department; Manuel, in a condo on East 61st Street, writing very real but moody novels and living—occasionally guiltily—on his wife's parents' money; and Tony (Antonio on his birth certificate) in Southhampton, designing houses and writing an occasional short story that always gets published, not because he knows everyone in the Hamptons but because the stories (actually, three is all) are really good.

I cannot say very much about Tony: I hate the Hamptons and will not go there, especially on the jitney where they pass out Perrier water to the elite. Consequently, I know him mostly through his stories. I suppose they are good; yes, they are, but the kind of stories—hep, hip, whatever—I would not read had not a relative written them. Only one of my sons—Manuel—is really like me in his single-minded devotion to literature, whatever that means, not a trace of his fatso evil mother in him, not a manipulative self-serving trait either. He gets invited to lecture and to PEN's literary gatherings, but stays home in his study, the only room in the condo without a spectacular view of the East River. I am including the many bathrooms.

Randy is not steadfast in his devotion to the arts, and I suspect he has inherited what Fatso called her planning-ahead talent, but he looks exactly like me, or, rather, what I looked like when all my juices were flowing. God knows, the juices flow in him: at least one affair with a student each term. But he knocks off—that is the right verb—an excellent short story or script or critical article without much effort whenever he can sit still long enough. One script got produced, bombed at the box office, as he proudly says, but developed a cult following in the more arcane video stores of the Village and the Upper West Side. He has been riding on that ever since; i.e. his job with NYU's graduate arts program.

That is enough for now about my sons.

I have not told any of them about my Death Sentence. Or anyone else, for that matter. In a steady voice, the urologist said, like a bureaucrat issuing driving instructions, there was no treatment that could prolong my life. There is nothing they can do—so why should I make anyone foolish enough to care for me suffer for the short time left? Who knows how long that short time is?

Three, four months? Why inconvenience them either? I think the boys all love me, but they have never been put to the test: I always pick up the check when we have lunch. Ha-ha!

Have I said that my surname is Morán? It sounds Irish, but it is, in fact, Spanish. I like the now-you-see-it-now-you-don't quality of it, and I am glad to have passed it on to the boys. Thank God, their fatso mother was not a radical feminist and did not insist on hyphenating her tacky name onto mine, whatever other hellishness she was and is capable of. Her name is... Oh, forget it, she's not a character in this story. Maybe not, but I'll take the chance and mention her only to denounce her. As it is, I think I may be flinging out too much information too quickly, too much for the reader to absorb. I hope he or she will not have to turn back to these pages later on and check out each name whenever a character reenters. I am not a character of course, but the others are: they are my version of the real people and that makes them characters. What the hell, let the reader turn back. I did with Tolstoy and Dostoevsky.

I have not told you my given name. Germán. The Nazis ruined it for me and for all who do not notice the accent mark. Not that in Spanish it means German or anything Teutonic. If it did, I'd go down to City Hall and do the needful. I don't think anyone has been named Adolf in sixty years. It's going to take longer to bring it back into usage than George after our revolution. No one really cares about any but his own name.

And yet the only fault I found with Thom, the fellow who calls me Dad, when we first more than nodded to one another was that he told me immediately how to spell his given name. And when he recited his surname—Abercrombie—he quickly added, "Not those Abercrombies—they were in trade!" But that's okay, for he explained in the next breath (as novelists used to say but don't anymore because their characters do not really breathe), "With a name like that I should aspire not only to be a director and playwright but the head of a foundation who escorts Brooke Astor and the editor of *Vogue* and such. But me, I'll end up only being a stage manager—that's because I'm a bossy busybody."

I laughed, although I felt sure he must have made that speech before, having myself prepared many before I fell asleep—alas, always too late to put them to use.

"Thanks, Dad," he said. He was small and looked up at me like a puppy. This was the first time he called me Dad. "You passed the test." He tilted his head to one side, imitating an ingenue. "You need an escort, you know." I decided he mostly wanted to be a director but had de-emphasized it from his self-introductory speech on the grounds of immodesty.

This encounter did not occur until just before the L.A. hiatus, but I'll explain about that later. Until then there was only one person on my floor I noticed—Gwendolyn. How can I describe her? She's Irish, but far removed; two generations of middle-class Irish Americans intervene and their emigration was not from Ireland but from Boston working-class neighborhoods. From Ireland, at least three generations. So far removed, indeed, to western Connecticut that the family's latest batch, Gwendolyn's nephews and nieces, confuse the IRA with investment bonds. All in her family are leery of both: anything decidedly old sod—another word they don't know—and any financial hedge that is not solid real estate, something you can go look at on an empty day. That last has been changed by a brother who got an MBA in business and tries to tell his skeptical siblings about mutual funds and debentures.

But Gwendolyn is not, of course, like them. She is an actress—an actor, she would say—of such seriousness, so intent on the nature of reality that she seems in the midst of her huge family close to sui generis. Too fancy, that. (Actually, I have only met two or three sisters singly.) I mean, she has come to her art on her own. I believe the Ireland suppressed by her family in America is erupting in her.

Let me explain. I love the Irish. There's a standard speech I give to fellow left wingers—particularly Jews—who have suffered at the hands and drunken speech of Irish Catholics in New York City. Where, I ask, would English literature be in the last century without the Irish? To glance only at the peaks: Wilde, Shaw, O'Casey in drama, Joyce in the novel, O'Connor in the short story, Yeats—ah, Yeats!—in poetry. And just below them—at this point Feltscher (that's the sculptor) once interrupted scornfully. He screeched, "Since when are you an anglophobe?"

He got it wrong, of course—if anything I am an anglophile—but I left it at that. I never did get to tell him, as I do my sons periodically, that my father (Rafael) came from the northwest of Spain. Galicia. The Celts at the height of their power seeped into that marvelous green corner of Spain. And knew enough then about sailing to cross over to Ireland to overwhelm it with their genes. Hundreds of years later, or maybe thousands, on my first visit to that island (as soon as Fatso got out of my way—but no more about her) also damp and green like my father's province, I stepped out of my modest hotel facing the Connolly railroad station in Dublin, the last Galician to make the crossing. (Did you get that?), a railroad station in a dismally Catholic country named after a militant socialist leader of the Easter uprising! That's a crazy gasping sentence, but I'll leave it that way: I was so agog in Dublin I could not have composed a sentence that would get past Fowler.

I stopped and stared at the drab station intently, but it would not tell me anything about Connolly. As soon as I took a step, I was stopped by an oldish woman who had crossed over from the station. Her speech was as sweet as Sara Allgood's and she asked me how to get to the O'Connell Bridge. I was stunned that she came to me for directions, but managed to smile when I realized what she saw in me—a tall, gray-haired man with black, bushy eyebrows, a typical old Dubliner heading for a pub. A tribute to the Celts that stayed back in Spain.

I had studied the street maps of Dublin for days before my flight and I could point her towards O'Connell, a short distance away. "I am going there meself, dear," I said, unflattening my vowels as much as I could on short notice. But despite the "meself" and the "dear," I did not fool her.

She tittered. "You're an American," she said, "from Boston, if you ask me." And laughed less constrainedly this time. "And a Kennedy, if you ask me twice!" She had bad teeth but wonderful checks and eyes, and as you can see, the verbal gift of the Irish.

"Ah," I said, "you've found out me secret, begorra."

But she was a country lady and she skittered away towards O'Connell, her shoulders hunched protectively, her rump generously protruding. I watched her a moment and she never looked back. A grand welcome. Joyce might have slyly smiled about my bubbling foolishness and forgiven me.

Of course, Irishness is not the reason I love Gwendolyn, though I admit it creates a predisposition. Yes, I do love Gwendolyn. I should say it and I do say to you who cannot ask me questions. I have not said it to Gwendolyn. I have returned her hugs, I have let her keep her head on my shoulder and her hands kneading mine; but I have never placed my hands on her breasts and I have never said that I love her with the concentrated wire-strong love of an old man.

First, I love her because she is blonde. She stays so for several weeks at a time, then her light brown hair begins to peek out between the two hundred-dollar dyeing sessions. Isn't that something? But she is an actress and she has got to do it, like paying rent. Housing should be as free as air and public parks. I have always believed that—it is one of the reasons I love the Cuban Revolution. But let's not get into that. Like me, it's wobbling around fatally wounded. What does this have to do with natural blonde hair? Nothing, but I warn you, if you stick with me, I shall stray: turn a page, I won't mind.

Another reason I love Gwendolyn is, she's not sharp-boned and skinny. Once she described an open audition she had gone to as a kind of slave auction. "We stood around eyeing one another and everyone was prettier and skinnier than the next." My hand does not sink into her flesh (she will never turn into a fatso as did you know who) when I cannot help but reach out and hold her arm. There is dear flesh there, not lonely sinews and bones.

Sometimes I pretend to close my eyes for a moment as if to give them a rest. I don't think she knows that I keep a slit open to look down at the apex of her legs under those light shifts she wears, that I am hoping to catch the outline of her little mound. It never occurs to me to do that with the elderly ladies, some as old as me, who also live in our small apartment building. What emanates from their invitations is a terrible loneliness, and I withdraw and look away. Whereas there is not mistaking what Gwendolyn makes me feel when she hugs an arm of mine as we walk towards Fifth Avenue or lifts a hand and lightly caresses my face and ends the gesture by smoothing down my eyebrows, as if that had been her motive, like me pretending to close my eyes all the way to rest them for a moment when I am, in fact, sneaking a look. Lovers are deceivers.

I am a writer and I cannot describe Gwendolyn's person the way practically every novelist does. Even my eccentric Ivy Compton-Burnett interrupts her tight dialogues to itemize what each speaker on entrance looks like; perfunctory, but she does it. What have I told you but that she is blonde and not skinny or fat? No other details, I notice. Unlike Edmund Wilson who in his journals, when older than I am now, goes so far as to betray his foot fetish time and again when he conscientiously describes a woman. My God, I realize now that I cannot say a word about Gwendolyn's feet. I must look at them closely next time. But I can talk at length about her hands and her collarbone. Enough.

She is a marvelous arrangement of flesh and bones and lightly freckled Irish epidermis.

◊

I always introduce myself to new tenants, as do the other old-timers, but Gwendolyn beat me to it. We were waiting for the elevator, and I thought, how nice, and nodded at her child. It was not love at first sight; she was merely pleasant to contemplate. For a month or so I helped her with packages while she maneuvered Owen's stroller and dug into a huge bag for keys. Each time she supplied me with one more bit of information, but never anything about the young man in her apartment. I remember asking myself, When did they move in?

"I shouldn't lock my door," she said the third time I walked her to it with her A & P bags. "Not in this building."

"Ah," I said, such a notion never having occurred to me—or to any of the old tenants in the building, I'm sure. "Ah," I repeated, somewhat dumbstruck, and we looked at one another and it was then I fell in love as in a summer movie release. There and then.

She felt something too, and she got up on her toes and pulled me down a little and kissed me on the right cheek. "Thanks," she said, grinned and once again went through all those darling motions and kissed me on the left cheek. "You're sweet."

She laughed with only a suggestion of sound—I guess she thought I was doing a double take—and her shoulders went up and down as she pushed Owen's stroller past the door jamb. She looked back at me and came over and took the bags. My mouth was agape. "Thanks," she said again, and this time her eyes glinted, but she did not kiss me a second time.

I stood there, still leaning over slightly as if waiting for another peck, and uttered not a word. It is not that I am shy, but women always bring me to a standstill in situations like this. Why shouldn't they? Situations like this don't happen often. She must have thought I hung back, but I did not, I was suspended, neither alighting nor in flight. She waved with one hand and let the door slam to behind her. I was in love; it certainly could not be lust: I've been inert since my second heart operation.

This happened towards the end of winter. My last winter, I told myself, surprised I had lived through it. I started peeking out every time I heard a noise in the hall, but each time I saw her, that young man was along. Finally, a week later, we met again at the elevator. She first looked intently at me after she said hello, and then segued into pleasantly studying me. I smiled foolishly.

"I was going to knock on your door," she said, "and tell you to watch *Law and Order* tonight."

"Oh?" I said. "I've never seen it. Is it good?"

"I'm in it," she said. "Tell me what you think—you're a writer. I try not to think if it's good, you know."

I said with enthusiasm, "That's wonderful. Forgive me, are there other things I should've seen you in?"

She shook her head.

"I'm an old number, you know," I said, hoping she would differ. "I don't know what's going on."

She waved a hand at shoulder height as if to wipe out what she had been tempted to say—something about my youthfulness, I wished—and instead came to the point tersely, "This is my big break."

"Congratulations," I said, and nodded and nodded, too shy, God knows why, to ask how she knew I was a writer.

She read my mind. "I found a book of yours in the library yesterday. I read fifty pages last night and then Owen woke up again."

I nodded and nodded again like a inept fifteen-year-old. Actually, I was thinking that I am right not to like children. Owen was gazing at me angelically at the moment. I could not smile benignly at him, as his look called for.

"It's a novel called *Jack*," she said.

"Oh, that one," I said, coming out of my trance.

"He's wicked," she said. "But I half like him."

I wished she had found the memoir of my Latino childhood. "Maybe you won't like him at all by the end," I said. About my own work I can always talk, and do. "That is, if you stay with it."

"I always stick with things I like," she said. "Or persons!"

And the elevator opened before I could be as bold. Out came Ernestine, a widow. More my speed than

Gwendolyn: old, but no Moms Mabley. She gave Gwendolyn a determinedly neutral look and said to me, "Gerry [that's what Germán has degenerated into] I came down to ring your bell."

Gwendolyn stepped into the elevator with Owen, and I meant to follow her, but Ernestine held me. "Have you been ill? You worry me," she said for Gwendolyn's ears. "I've been wanting to ask your advice."

The elevator door closed behind Gwendolyn and my heart descended with it.

Ernestine wanted to know what book she should buy her grandson for Christmas. He was fourteen. "I want to encourage him to read," she said, and looked at me as rapt as teenagers at Frankie in the old days. Fake, of course. I know about single old ladies: always on the prowl. I'm not flattered by their attention.

"*Huckleberry Finn*," I said like a shot, and took the stairs at the end of the hall, but I got down to the lobby too late. I almost sprinted to the sidewalk. I can't really do that anymore; I look like a kangaroo. Where did she and Owen go? I went east. My heart banged against my ribs. I decided to continue as far as University Place instead of turning down Fifth Avenue, but I found I was too short of breath to hurry. I gave up, stopped on the corner of Fifth and looked up and down. No Gwendolyn. I strolled with stiff legs, like every other old man, towards Washington Square.

Randy sat at the plate-glass window of the restaurant facing a corner of the park, looking for me but also showing off, and said without any greeting, "What's the matter with you?"

"Nothing," I said. "Why don't you ask that when I'm fine?"

He laughed and stood and slapped my shoulder—he's very Latin when it comes to physical contact—and then I realized my reply did not make sense. I relaxed.

"So?" I said.

"Don't ask about the novel," he said. "I don't have time to write these days. Okay?"

"I never ask," I said. "I know you're a swinging academic bureaucrat. You look it, too." He was dressed for the East Village. "I prefer tweeds, and a pipe to ponder with."

"That's not true," he said. "You know that."

"What?" I still had Gwendolyn on my mind and every thought went to her as soon as I stopped speaking.

"It's not true," he said.

"What?" I repeated.

"That you don't ask about my writing," he said. "I'm glad you do. It reminds me of my true mission. I think I made a mistake with this chairmanship, Papi."

Randy always uses that Latin-Americanism for Dad when he wants my sympathy, or maybe it's his way of thanking me for picking up the tab for lunch. He is the most consciously Latino of the boys. After the Columbia strike, he had hung around the Young Lords in the Barrio for a while, but he couldn't hope to be a leader there as he had been at the university. The Lords were friendly enough—he slept with a couple of the girls—but it finally got through to him that he did not really fit: he was not Puerto Rican or working class. Of course, some of the Young Lords' leaders are now talk-show hosts and

Daily News columnists, so there is no reason for Randy to be self-conscious when he calls me Papi.

And as for me, I don't mind it a bit, not one bit. Let Papi become as American as vamoose. I may look like an old Irish geezer, but my heart is in Galicia and Spain as well as Havana, where my Cuban grandfather came from two years after the Civil War. I made this last statement a year ago in the presence of some of Randy's students, and I could tell they thought I was a fraud—how could a living American standing in front of them use the Civil War as a personal reference point? I marvel at it myself.

I have become garrulous. Prolix, intellectuals used to say in the days when I aped them. You see? I always add something to a statement. Garrulous would have been enough, but I am always reminded of something else, in this case prolix. It's not that I eschew minimalism, I am merely old, that's all. Too old.

Which, of course, took me back to Gwendolyn, and I again lost track of Randy's conversation. Which I could take for granted was the sort of unending whining writers enjoy. I'm absurd, I said to myself, an old man falling in love with a young woman no older than his granddaughter. I looked at the menu as a kind of cover for my thoughts. Love like that only happens in movies and plays of the forties, and I was never convinced that they were not a hoax. For one thing, Herbert Marshall was their idea of an old man. A romantic limp he had, not prostate cancer, not even jock itch.

"You're not listening," Randy said.

"You've become prolix," I accused. Shift right into attack; I learned that from Fatso.

"What's that?" he asked, and meant it.

"Spend more time with the OED," I said, "and not with...you know."

"I should never tell you my troubles," he said. But he had a sense of humor and he smiled at what he had called his troubles.

Later, in fact after lunch, he asked, "What *is* prolix?"

I told him without being prolix—ha-ha!

Randy was a big fellow with a deep chest, and I could hear him exhale; you could call it a sigh of relief if you like clichés. He said, "I was afraid it meant something sexy."

I grunted and held him back from crossing Fifth Avenue against the light. He was walking me home because he had not finished talking, he thought, about the traits his wife lacked.

"I don't mind overwriting," he said. "I can always cut out the fat—but sex, it bugs me. You can't edit it, you can't take it back..."

"This family is excessively literary," I said, taking my usual tack with the boys.

"Cut it out," he said, and took my elbow to show his affection.

"What did you think prolix meant?" I said. "Some act in the Kama Sutra?'

He removed his hand from my elbow and placed it on my shoulder. "You're too young for that kind of talk," he said with a little push: he was careful of my frail bones. "My friend Saul can't believe it when I tell him..."

And that is when he met Gwendolyn for the first time. In front of my building, under the canopy, away from the sun so that the blue of her eyes and the pink of her complexion were not washed out. She did not look in Randy's direction, but I could tell, I could tell indeed. There were vibes there. I had to introduce them. I preferred listening to what his friend Saul, the erstwhile Hollywood baby mogul, thought of my avuncular sallies—and that's saying a lot.

I mumbled their names, and Gwendolyn glanced at Randy only once and then for a mere second, and without a pause turned her blue eyes on me in a sweet, caring manner I had not seen her use with anyone else but Owen. I studied her eyes to see if there was something new in them, and it hurt to look. Randy's image might well still be reflected in them. I couldn't tell. Once long ago I felt that such a thing had happened. Who was the girl then? Could it have been Fatso? Never. Whoever she was, her image stayed in the pupils of my eyes—don't ask me for proof—after she had passed from my ken. Now it was a different story and it caused me anguish to look for Randy in Gwendolyn's eyes.

"Don't forget," she said. "Let me know what you think." She nodded in Randy's direction and started inside. For a moment she seemed to expect me to follow her.

I did not, because Randy held me at the elbow again.

"What's her name again, by the way?" he asked.

"Costello," I said. "By the way."

"Italian?" he said, stalling for time.

"Costello is an old Irish name," I said.

"Oh," he said.

"That's the kind of thing a New York writer should know," I said. I shook his hand off. "Thanks for lunch—or did I pay?"

"Wait," he said.

"If you want to see her again, watch *Law and Order* tonight," I said.

"Hey, stop," he called after me. "I wanna ask you something."

On the step of the doorway, still under the canopy, I turned around and said, "Next time, the lunch is on you."

"Really?" he said, and started towards me.

"Really," I said, grimaced, and added, "You're so stingy you're getting to be a freeloader."

He shrugged that off and said, "I mean about *Law and Order*. Is she really on it?"

I nodded. I hope I did not pale, but he knew that I knew that something had happened, although he did not know the whole of it. My involvement, that is. I left him there looking like a big lug. I had never seen him in heat before.

In the elevator, the dire musical strophes from the last act of *Carmen*, presaging tragedy, crashed over my head. For the first time in my life I held a hand to my heart. Proust had his little musical phrase, fey as hell, and in a string quartet to boot; I need brasses and drums and the shrill crowd outside the bullring to shatter me. I could have crumpled to the floor, but my knees held. Upstairs I walked out the elevator, shoulders thrown back, heroically: it takes me a long time to recall how ordinary and uninflatable all the denouements of my life eventually turn out to be. Farce. If I were in the audience, I would laugh at me. Does this displacement show in my writing? Am I writing low comedy, not tragedy? Ah, that would be a tragedy, indeed.

◇

I lowered myself carefully to the Kennedy rocker in my living room, and many thoughts and emotions rushed into my head, like stormy waters into a small cove. There is so much I have to say these days that normal conversations cannot accommodate, and so many emotions to sift that I have to sit down and rock to do them justice. I wish I kept a journal to let myself go. As I told you, I don't have one. Just a listing each day in a notebook called *Daily Reminder*; a diary, you could say. I never kept a journal either in the days when I published. I don't need to muse in prose about literature or politics or the vagaries of the people that brush against me. These days I would not muse, I would rail. I admit I wish there were one person to tell everything to. I want at least one living being on my side. Lacking that, a journal will have to do. Are you reading me now?

One such confession: that thing I said about always knowing what's not true, I'll come clean: I have four CD's worth ten thousand each and another fifty thousand in mutual funds. It's all I've got to show.

I panted a little. What a thing to talk about...how bourgeois can you get. What would my Cuban grandfather have thought of me? I forgot—I also get $810 each month from Social Security, something Abuelo was not a beneficiary of. He died at seventy-eight when a car hit him. I was overseas during the war, and it has not occurred to me until now to find out what he did for pocket money. Abuelo lived in Tampa with my sister and a female cousin and their husbands. Oh, it must have been difficult to slip him a ten, he was such a proud man. He never even had a savings account; I know because I remember the run on the Ybor City Bank when I was ten. We kids could go anywhere we wanted (I don't know whether we were allowed; we didn't ask, we just did it) and Mario and I hurried up to Seventh Avenue and looked at the people milling about on the corner of 19th Street.

Abuelo played bolita, five or ten cents each day, and he won two or three times every year. Little amounts, of course, but before he went to bed he always spent his winnings on the family or gave it away to his grandchildren. That's how I got to see the Ringling Brothers Circus when I was seven.

I have another reason for telling you all this. I learned it from Balzac; after him, every novelist feels an obligation to tell you where his characters get their money. If he doesn't do it, it is a conscious choice. A guilty choice, I hope. I always want to know how the dramatis personae make a living or if they don't have to. It stops me dead in a story if I don't immediately get a hint at least. I have to know even when it's Cary Grant in a romantic comedy. Watch out for a writer who is not forthcoming about money; it means that money is primarily on his mind.

I knew what was primarily on mine. I moved to the Queen Anne's chair that faces the TV set as if I were going to turn it on, but I knew that I was prevaricating, delaying, stalling, with all that stuff about Balzac and Abuelo. I was ashamed to diagnose myself as sick with love, and I am loath to say it now. My stomach clutched a hardball inside it that I could not jostle or I would lose my lunch. I thought I knew about love and I am not implying that until Gwendolyn came along I was ignorant of it. I knew all that was needful. What I did not know is the effect it can have on an old body. The ball shifted and I placed a hand over my mouth.

I settled for a groan. I looked at the apartment door. No one came to it; there were no calls for me to open up. The building was a solid one, built in the 1920's; no one would hear me. I allowed myself another moan.

After a while, I felt I could reach for the remote control without upsetting the boat. The TV was set to the Sports Channel and an afternoon game at Shea Stadium came on, between the Mets and the Braves. The players all looked so healthy and young I almost turned it off. The game turned into a duel between Saberhagen and Glavine. They were perfectly matched, not like me and Randy. Two infield errors gave the Mets three runs, and Glavine did not show the slightest chagrin. But in the eighth, Dallas Green stupidly gave Saberhagen a rest and we lost the game. Moral: never let down your guard.

I don't know, maybe there is no moral; maybe it's a wayward world.

When the ball game ended, near the time I always give myself a second injection of insulin, I moved over to my desk and summed up the events of the day in my *Daily Reminder*. I write this always during the same time of day, more or less, when Virginia Woolf, just before tea, added her spiteful entries to her journal, not *Daily Reminders* bought at a Sixth Avenue store but fancy notebooks that Leonard had them make up for her at the Hogarth Press. No lousy comparisons, please. I wrote: *Did not fall asleep until 3am. Ibuprofen & Ambien finally worked. Breakfast, read Times, thought of an angle for an Op-Ed piece on Cuba, wrote opening paragraph. Met Randy for lunch. Fourth Street restaurant in midst of NYU. Ran into Gwendolyn Costello; says she will be on TV tonight. Mrs. Puglia asked me to recommend a gift book for her grandson. Mets lost to Braves 4-3; Shaberhagen and Glavine. Spent $29.50 for lunch, including tip.*

Tomorrow I will write that I watched *Law and Order*, but not that I went over to her apartment and paused just long enough to compose my compliments before I rang the doorbell. Nor will I say that I heard them quarreling. Her young man had a powerful voice and hers projected rather well, too. Curses, maledictions, obscenities: opera. I thought better of it—that is, embarrassing them with my presence—and went back to my place. It does not go into my diary: I was not part of it. I didn't hear what their fight was about and no one on my floor saw me out in the hall. What could they be fighting about? Was it just the usual fight between married people? Like Fatso and me—not that I ever yelled; our fights were mostly embittered silences that wore my molars down.

I sat again in the living room and tried to get over my foolishness. It then occurred to me that my painful physical reaction that afternoon was caused by my cancer spreading. The old DS. Of course. What a relief that this is what it likely was. I laughed. I had taken the right cure unthinkingly—codeine with Tylenol, or a No. 3 as they say on the street—and I was now feeling okay. I went over to the word processor and looked at the paragraph on Cuba. It wouldn't make a difference, whatever I wrote; I'd just be one of the blatherers, Right or Left.

The phone rang and I figured it was Randy. It was. I listened to him leave a message on the machine. I didn't pick it up. I felt a pang in my stomach at the sound of his voice. There went my cancer theory. I was jealous, like a young buck. "Hey, your neighbor was good," he said cheerily. "I'll call you tomorrow, Papi." And no doubt he would.

◇

Next morning I picked up the phone as soon as it rang. Ordinarily, I don't do that until about eleven; I'm not a civilized person before that hour. But I decided I might as well be done with delays and met my old man's fate head-on. It was not Randy, it was Billie Gladiola. My God, how come?

"Billie, I'm sorry..." I said, "about your husband." I had forgotten his name and those of his two predecessors. Semyon? No, he had been a lover. "I heard too late..."

"Life goes on," she said, always ready with a cliché. "We must hang on, Gerry. They need us to carry on."

"Yes, yes," I said, and wondered if more than one man in her life had died lately; the other husbands had evaporated.

"It's a tough world," she said. "You and me, we can take it. We're survivors."

Another fake truism out of her mouth and I would vomit. Why did I always let her get away with that kind of stuff? No other male would have. I made some more noises. I could not run away the way I always did when I ran into her in the West Village. The last time was during the Desert War; she was leading her girls, all as weathered as she, down Seventh Avenue, with the dwarfish Avila Tumac beating a drum at her side, slowly, mournfully. Bong, bong, bong—I am sure that the Incas were never that lugubrious. Billie forced me to fall behind her. Avila whispered to me, "Billie wants us to go east on Bleecker and then up Sixth," but I slipped away at Sheridan Square.

The group was comprised of some sixteen women and a couple of squashed males. Their dumb procession in our liberal neighborhood, of course, protested the war. Billie is older than I, no one knows exactly how much. (I once made Fatso very angry—she was a fan of Billie's for a short while—because I called Billie One Hundred Years of Public Solicitude. Not bad, huh?) As far as I know, she never took a wrong political stand. She is a conservationist, a vegetarian, a pacifist, a philosophical anarchist. All societies are bad for you and ours especially. How could you go wrong with such a program? That she could traipse around of a Saturday morning with those old girls was proof that ours is an open society, something she would not want to prove. Nor I, for that matter. In the Village it was a self-indulgence. Harmless nonsense. The Desert War was over for all practical purposes. Our boys were now being exposed only to that rash which later on became a front page story for one day.

"Gerry, it is good to hear your voice, kid," she said, never relaxing her gum-chewing shtick delivery to show her working-class origins. Actually, her folks had owned a medium-size dry goods store in Cincinnati. They lived upstairs, but kept a second home on the lake. And Billie went to Bennington. "I want you to lend it to a gathering they want me to put together today. It will mean a lot to them. Me, too."

"Billie..." I began with a no-thank-you tone. "You know I..."

"Gerry, I know, you're a very private guy," she said. "That's why I love you—we're the same."

I was too nonplussed to reply. That woman always wins.

"This is a little get-together for Shukovsky," she continued, a weary, tolerant note in her voice, as if for her, too, the whole thing was a duty her good heart would not allow her to shirk. And she actually added, "A duty, kiddo."

Not for me, I could shirk it. "Shukovsky?" I said.

"The Ukrainian short-story writer."

"That sounds like a Russian name to me." It was the best I could think of to get out of it, but I knew—not too deep within me—it would not be good enough for Billie.

"You know Stalin tried to colonize all the other nations with Russians," she said, and emitted a hard little working-class laugh. "I was never an anti-communist, but you know how Uncle Joe was."

If I held out any longer, she would call me an old Stalinist and not be far off the mark. I gave in and promised to be at her place in the afternoon. As soon as I said this she added that afterwards we would all walk over to the New School for a little public gathering in one of their lecture halls. "It's all very proper and bourgeois this time, Gerry," she ended, which I hope meant we would not be accompanied by a mind-destroying drumbeat. I don't mean to sound paranoid, but she was also saying that I had become very proper, the sort of bourgeois who would not follow her and her girls down Seventh Avenue: Billie gets you coming or going.

There was no time to fulminate about her. The moment she was through with me the phone rang again. This time it was Randy. He still sounded cheerful.

"What if I get some lunch and bring it over? You brew some coffee for us and we'll be comfy."

"Brew? I don't brew—never mind. What time is it?"

"I don't mean now. In a couple of hours. Anything special or do you leave it to me?"

I thought: I'm dying, why should I busy myself with anything else?

"It won't cost you a penny. I heard what you said yesterday. You know money's never on my mind. I don't notice who pays."

I exhaled loudly. "Okay, but I'm not brewing any coffee. Get it in paper cups, if you have to."

"We never finished talking yesterday," he said in his cool way, as if he were the parent. "We'll have a good chat."

All of it a cover-up. I knew why he wanted to come over. It was he who had made me sick yesterday. Yes, it was he, not Gwendolyn. I checked on my stomach while he talked, but it was not ailing. I touched it. Was I over the whole thing already? I'd know when next I saw Gwendolyn.

"I did," I said. "I don't have anything more to say on the subject. If you don't already know what I think about how a writer who doesn't..."

"Save that for later," he said. "I like it when you criticize me. I take it to heart. It's good for me."

"I'll see you—bring whatever," I said, in better spirits than when I finished with Billie.

There was a tap on the door. Why didn't they ring?

"I didn't want to ring," Gwendolyn said, "in case you were sleeping."

The pang came right back.

I was saved by the bell, as we used to say about boxers wearily open for a knockout blow. It was the phone again. I managed to wave Gwendolyn inside before I turned away to answer it. I kept my back to her once she was in. A natural stance, it would seem, when you answer the phone in my place, but in fact I did not want her to see my dismay. More fright than dismay, but I could not control either.

It was Randy. "I forgot to ask," he said. "If you're having someone in, I can bring lunch for him, too."

Him, indeed. His slight pause to keep himself from saying "her" brought me back to normal. I said, "Who do you think I am—Perle Mesta?"

"Who's that?" he asked, but I did not tell him. "Well, if that should change," he said, "just call me, okay?"

"No!" I said emphatically. "I'm not making coffee either—you bring that." I could hear him saying I had already said that as I hung up on him.

I turned back to her. There she was. She grinned; I relaxed. She looked darling, also expectant. She really likes me, I thought, and then I remembered *Law and Order*.

I said, "I forgot I haven't told you about the show," and her eyes froze with the fearful expectation every artist feels when someone is about to tell him what he thinks of the performance, the painting, the book. "You were wonderful," I said. "You added a note of reality to every scene you were in."

She brought a hand to her heart. "You don't mean that," she said, and of course completely believed me. "What a wonderful thing to say."

"The note of reality, you mean?" I said, flattered.

She nodded, up and down two or three times. "You said wonderful too, but that about reality..."

I said, "It's just a fact."

"That's because you're a writer—that you can speak so beautifully," she said, and took her hand from her heart and placed it, palm out, on her forehead. "I haven't any writer to speak to. Well, playwrights and they're..." She let that peter out and somehow made it sound expressive.

"Even though you were called on to make us believe you were undergoing things beyond your experience," I said.

She had played a pregnant young woman trying to get off drugs, desperately cleaning and scrubbing and polishing her tiny apartment in the East Village, her way of detoxifying. She had been both filthy and endearing, a hardworking but incompetent housekeeper and, when her blue eyes looked directly into the camera, heartbreaking.

She reached out and touched my arm. "Well, I did have Owen."

"But there were other details..."

"I know what you mean." She pressed my arm as she said it. "How was it you put it? A note of reality?"

I was now so at ease that I said, "You want to drag this out, is that it?"

She covered her eyes with one hand to show shame. "Tell me, tell me what I did wrong," she pled. "I have so much to learn."

I was no fool. We don't need to hear what we...we artists, that is...do wrong; we know that only to well. It is what we do well that we need confirmed.

"You did everything right." I made a circle with forefinger and thumb and held it up to shoulder height.

"Oh, oh!" She looked about her. "I have to sit down. I am fainting." She took my hand and drew me down next to her on the couch. "Are you telling me the truth?"

"No," I said.

She laughed. "God, you're sweet."

We sat silent a moment. I raised my eyes and saw through the kitchen doorway the dirty dishes piled in the sink. I could not think of a thing to say. That is, I was thinking of a number of things, but they were not sayable.

"What about the moment when she discovers he's on the drug squad?" She looked sideways as if she expected a blow and did not want to get the full impact. "Remember that part?"

I did not. "You made it very real," I said. "It was very badly written."

"Written?"

"The whole story was a cliché," I said.

"You're right," she quickly agreed, and she let go my hand in order to express herself freely. "It's so difficult to find the truth of a moment like that, I mean, when the writer is falling back on... as you said."

I stopped looking at her breasts and I got my bearing. "I meant to ring your bell last night and congratulate you, but someone called and kept me on."

"Your son?" she said politely.

I nodded slowly and kept my eyes on her. "I have two others, you know."

"How wonderful!" she said. "Three sons."

"Writers," I said, lumping them all and waiting to see if she was going to get specific. I did not allow myself to wonder what she was getting at when she asked if it was Randy who called. I had no intention of lumping *her* beforehand into the category of waitresses who keep refilling his coffee cup before he has barely sipped from it. Who am I fooling with this disclaimer—of course, I wondered, indeed, feared the worst.

"All three?" she said.

I nodded.

"Including the one I saw yesterday?"

She was zeroing in. I did not want to put her to the test, but I did. I told her what each did, but concentrated mostly on Tony, adding nothing about Randy except to cast him as a husband and father.

I finished my peroration on Tony with, "He's an architect but cannot fight off his literary talent."

"Oh," she said, and I was certain she would lead me back to Randy.

"Tony is a very good architect," I said. "I wish he wouldn't mess up his life with literature."

She didn't get it. Instead, a little sigh escaped her, and she sat forward in the couch. She was giving up on Randy, I thought. Maybe I was wrong about her and him, but never about him and any hers.

"There were two things I really came to see you about," she said. "First, I stayed up very late and finished your book last night. I loved it, I laughed so much and felt so sad, too."

She said a few more things like that, as if she had come backstage after the performance to pay her respects to a friend in the cast. I wanted her to say more, of course, but my years have taught me not to show it.

Unlike her. She was certainly much better, more articulate than those who would say brightly, "I read your book," and no more, having paid you what they think is the supreme compliment. She ended with a charming gesture; she held one hand over her heart and made it flutter, like a heroine in a silent movie.

I said, "So you didn't come to hear what I thought of your performance?"

She folded over as only the young can do, and laughed on the way up. "I knew you'd be wicked! I'm going to have to watch my step. I'm only an actor, and you know what they say about us."

"What?"

"That we're dumb..."

"Ho-ho," I said, but she was right: they are dumb. "And what was the second reason?"

"I've forgotten!" She blinked and her eyes brightened and stayed on me, establishing the most astonishing intimacy. I suppose actresses can do that as easily as produce tears. "I've forgotten, would you believe it?"

"I do," I said, and I was in danger of losing my breath if I continued to return her gaze. "That happens often to old people. We forget from minute to minute."

"You're not old," she said in a murmur, and laid her head on my shoulder. "Not old at all."

I placed a hand on her hair. It was silky. I looked at it. My hand was stringy and mottled. Not right.

The doorbell rang. I took my hand away. This was melodrama. She looked up, but did not remove her head. She made a circle of her lips. "Oh?" she whispered.

"Excuse me," I said. I got up and felt relieved that our love scene was cut short. Why hadn't the doorman announced this visitor? I walked towards the tiny foyer with my head turned to look at Gwendolyn, as if checking that she was decent. I expected it was Ernestine still in pursuit and, for a moment, considered not opening the door. Rather my darling Gwendolyn, of course, than Ernestine with her eternal invitations to dinner: pasta was so easy to prepare and yet so delicious, come. One can think of a thousand things in the five paces it takes to arrive at my apartment door: I rejected Ernestine again and again before I got there.

It was Randy, filling the doorway in that bulldozer way of his.

"A student canceled," he explained. "I thought I'd come over early."

The fool thought the look on my face was simple surprise. "Oh," I said.

"There's so much I want to discuss..." He stopped. He saw Gwendolyn and his whole stance changed: he turned into a snake mesmerizing a rabbit—you know, the high-class brand of violence pornography that PBS sneaks into its programming.

That may be an exaggeration, but it's what I thought as he bore down on me. I was so convinced he'd gobble her down that in my rattled way I started to introduce them to divert him. Quite formally, too.

"We've met, Dad," he said (was he reminding her I am old?) and moved quickly around me into the living room. He bent over her. "Hello," he said, and first looked at her with his wonderful smile spreading across his face and ended with his intense, intimidating gaze—right into her eyes—still hovering.

And right before me I saw Gwendolyn become fragile. She sank into the sofa. She reminded me of Lilian Gish in *Birth of a Nation*—that's how old I am. And I felt even older watching what is now called their body language. Whereas Gish cringed from that big brute of a black in that unashamed whole-heartedly racist scene, Gwendolyn did not so much draw away as entice Randy forward. His feet moved towards her and then back like a runner working up before the starting gun.

Go ahead, laugh at me; the two of them were breaking my heart. I wanted them to leave. I was on the verge of a fatigue headache, a gift of my DS. My DS! I had not thought about it for two days. The thundering chords of *Carmen* again crashed over my old head.

I was sitting down when I came to.

"You've been in front of a camera before? I ask because of our student films," he was saying.

Randy was sitting, too. On the sofa next to Gwendolyn. He continued talking, but for me it was a dumb show. He gestured like a Latin and I knew where those big hands wanted to light on. I dug my feet into the rug to keep from sliding to the floor and felt myself slowly moving away from the center of my consciousness.

But nothing was real, not even my losing consciousness. What in fact happened was that catch-all of a banal phrase: my head swam—but did not sink. Randy brought me to shore. He was standing again. Had I really seen him on the sofa in that hunched fucking position? I should not put it so crudely, but that is what my battered mind made of the image, mirage or not.

"Dad, I've got a proposition," he said.

I daresay.

"Oh, sweetheart," Gwendolyn called out to me. "Are you all right?"

"Yes, of course," I replied coolly, putting her in her place.

Undeterred, Randy continued as if no one had spoken, taking no notice of my pallor and palpitations. "What say if I go down and bring up lunch for all of us? I'll take your orders." He half-turned towards Gwendolyn and I gathered this was the first time he had made the proposal. "Don't say no—it's no trouble," he said sideways to me and then turned all the way in her direction. "And it'll be a lot of fun."

Gwendolyn gave him a brilliant smile, not the natural beguiling sweet one she always directed at me. This smile is an actressy one, I said to myself, grabbing at straws; but she did look my way with a more real Irish-girl concern, having forgiven me for snubbing her. She got up and took my hand, prudently, however, as might a nurse taking my pulse. "Better?" she asked.

"Fine," I said, and this was true.

"Why?" Randy asked. "Are you sick?"

I laughed; he will ask me that when I am on show in my coffin. "I'm fine, but, . . ." the idea came to me mid-sentence, "the two of you, why don't you go out and have lunch. I'll stay here; I need to rest."

"Why?" Randy asked again. He turned to Gwendolyn this time. "Is he sick?"

"I'm fine," I said, "but I've got a busy afternoon ahead and I..."

"Oh, okay," Randy said, easily allowing lunch with Gwendolyn to supersede any worries. "Have it your way."

Nothing replaced my own worries. I was testing her by suggesting they go out to lunch. Would she go with Randy? Had she succumbed? My heart thumped like Disney's rabbit.

Gwendolyn said nothing; she gave my hand a squeeze and went to the door. Randy followed. A terrible moment. She looked back. "Later," she began, then pressed her lips together as if calculating what to say. "All right?..."

I put off the moment of truth with a question. I said "Where's Owen?" and controlled the quaver in my voice.

"With my friend Susan and her little girl," she said, and I saw her come to a decision. She would tell me now, and she waved a hand weakly, ruefully to keep my attention. "I never got to tell you the second reason I came over. We're going to L.A. on Friday."

I groaned. "Oh, God, that's in two days," I said as if it were bad news, and it was, and I did not care that Randy was there. "Go on, go on." I myself waved them towards the door.

Randy said, "He *is* sick."

"It's only for two months, at most three," she explained.

The sound I made then is what I suppose is called keening. I was tempted to say that in three months I should be dead. But neither knew about my DS. I didn't have the energy to go into all that. "Go on," I repeated.

"My agent insists," she continued. "It's the casting season."

Randy forgot about me and pointed a finger at her. "As I said, I want to talk to you about appearing in our students' films—some of them get to be quite..."

Through my stunned, foggy haze I saw Gwendolyn respond to that. She turned to him in an actressy but eager fashion.

I managed to say, "What...what season?"

Later on, when I was put in possession of all the details, so to speak, I had to admit that Randy had been quick on the uptake. "Dad, every spring all the actors show up in L.A.," he said, "like salmon upriver." What was not funny was that he did go out the door with Gwendolyn when I kept insisting I was fine. But that's what I told them to do, wasn't it?

◇

In time I calmed down. In time I got up and went to the other room and lay down on my wide, welcoming bed. In time one gets over everything. And other such maxims, pseudo truths you find in Oxford University Press anthologies and Chinese fortune cookies. They lulled me to sleep. I awoke with difficulty—these days I seldom want to come out of the anesthesia of sleep—and I sat on the edge of the bed and remembered too soon that I was due at Billie Gladiola's in an hour. That was trouble enough for now.

To my surprise, when I rang Billie's bell, it was Thom, the boy on my floor, who answered. He looked different. He wore shiny black pants, a white ruffled shirt, and an expectant do-come-in look meant for whomever rang the bell. This was a diversion. Life inevitably perks one up.

"Hello?" I said, and smiled for the first time in hours.

He leaned forward almost into my arms. He exclaimed, "I knew you were distinguished!"

"I don't know about that," I said. "Don't tell me you're Billie's son."

He managed to say two things at once, like my darling you know who. He bugged his eyes to say God no, and replied to my demurrer at the same time. "Literary," he said. "A writer, right? I know from Gwendolyn. And the doormen. *You*'re distinguished."

I felt a returning pang at the sound of her name. But faint now. I said, "You a writer, too?"

He shook his head.

"Good," I said, and looked over his head (he was a little fellow) to the busy living room. "You don't wanna be that."

He explained with a sober look, "Today I work for a caterer."

"Caterer?" I said.

"I open the door, give people napkins." He half-laughed. "But I don't hand out dips. Girls do that." He shrugged. "Other days I'm really a—well, a theater worker."

"Theater worker?" I said, pleased.

"I'm no dummy," he said, "I've read Brecht."

I wanted to say something approving, a Stalinist do-good encourage-the-youth hangover, but Billie's voice called from the open double doors of this downstairs living room. (Oh, yes, there was also an upstairs sitting room, as in a Jane Austen novel.) "Hey, come on in," she said in her proletarian manner. She wore a genuine African dashiki—quite dashing, actually—and gestured me towards her. (We were on the street level of two floors of a Georgian townhouse her first husband gave her—rather, that she snatched from him when they divorced. She rented out the upper floors, and I've always wondered if she personally collected the rent each month.) "You're a brick to come," she said, and put her arm through mine with all the savoir faire of an experienced hostess. She gave Thom a look that made him scurry into the kitchen at the back end of the entrance way.

"See you, Thom," I called, and explained to her, "He lives in my building—he's in the theater."

"Yeah, he's a good kid," she said, although I'm sure she hadn't seen him before this afternoon. "You know, PEN sends these people to help, especially with me. You know me, I wouldn't know how to entertain anybody."

"I don't either," I said.

She leaned her head against me, but she is no Gwendolyn. "God, it's good to be with an old comrade like you, instead of..." and she gestured towards the guests.

"Where's this Shukovsky?" I said. "Let's see if I can entertain him."

"Be careful," she said, and snapped her chewing gum. "I don't think he's an old comrade of anybody."

She still had a good head on her, even if it didn't feel good on my shoulder. Ha-ha. But you know what I mean—politically, that is. Her heart is another matter.

"I'll say something equivocal about Jews," I said, "and see if he rises to the bait."

She tapped my arm. "Cut it out," she said, in case I really meant to rock the boat.

I checked the side pockets of my jacket to see if I carried a codeine number 3. (I tuck them into all my outer wear now.) One was lodged in a tiny inner pocket. If I took it, then no liquor. Which deadening agent did I prefer?

"If PEN is supplying the liquor, I want a bourbon," I said. "I don't want any cheap stuff."

"You're not just a good, old comrade," she said, "you're a good, ole boy."

I remembered now what I liked about her. "Hey, you must be tanked up already," I said, and gave her arm a mostly genuine squeeze against my hip.

She nudged that particular elbow up into my side and muttered, "What the hell, like you said, it's not my booze they're guzzling."

I gave her another squeeze to encourage her in her truth-telling jag.

"Here," she said, and took her arm away to point to one side of the wide door in the living room.

Sunk in an easy chair sat Shukovsky. You would know him anywhere—a boyar in an Eisenstein movie, crude and powerful, dumb and wily. He was an up-to-date version; he wore one of those shiny suits popular with Italian squares fifteen years ago. A different tour that must have been for him, a different Establishment, too.

Billie brushed aside a couple of people. "Shukovsky," she called, as if she had stepped into a barnyard. "This is Gerry Morán. I mean, Germán, God. He's a..."

"A novelist," he said, and I won't try to reproduce his accent. "The novelist?"

Somebody must have filled him in.

Billie said, "He introduced Latinos into American literature."

And we were all stuck with that, including the two eager ones who had been hovering over Shukovsky, professional literary PR persons who make up the rank and file of these gatherings. They nodded in agreement, but of course said nothing. Shukovsky gaped. What could anyone say to her description of me?—a historical icon is a historical icon. What could Billie herself have added to it?

She waved a hand at a pretty girl going by with a tray of dirty glasses. "Bring us some drinks."

The girl stopped and waited for more instructions with that bright open-eyed look that, I decided, they must teach all young actresses now. Again, I thought of Gwendolyn, and my heart turned over. Maybe I should take the number 3 instead?

Billie stared right back at the girl as at a rival, then said stentoriously, "Bourbon. What about you, Shukovsky? More vodka?"

"No, no," he said with alacrity. "Scotch and water."

Billie pointed to me and said, “Bourbon for him. I’m not drinking.”

Ha-ha, but I said nothing. She waved the girl away like a vulgar bourgeois.

Shukovsky winked at me. “I introduce Scotch in Russian literature.”

I said, “Vodka a lot of other fellows took care of.”

Shukovsky twirled his bushy mane and looked up at the ceiling. “Aiee, aiee,” he said. “Not only in literature.”

“What’re you talking about?” Billie said, and half-turned towards the rest of the room, as if threatening to leave us. “Huh?”

I said, “Run with the ball, Billie.”

Shukovsky liked that, too. He laughed like a baritone in Mussorgsky. “Is very witty, New York,” he said. He nodded and his mane came forward. He looked at Billie to include her in his compliment.

“Yeah,” Billie said.

I shook my head. “No,” I said.

“No?” Shukovsky said, surprised. “Everybody tell me that.”

“It’s me who’s witty,” I said. “Anybody you hear say something funny is copying me.”

Mussorgsky again.

“What is this?” Billie protested. “Some kind of macho scene?” And she wasn’t kidding.

Shukovsky was puzzled, but he did not let it stop him from what he wanted to say. “In fancy restaurant my host says to the maitre, he say, What’s the damage?”

We waited to hear the rest.

"He means the bill!" Shukovsky said, and threw one arm up. I thought he held up the arm like an exclamation point, but he was, in fact, reaching for the Scotch and water. He sipped. "In New York is only good Scotch."

I took my bourbon. I said, "You sure you don't want this, Billie?"

"Later," she said, but I don't think she knew what she was replying to. "We go from here to the New School." She nodded as if I had asked a question, as if sagacity were a burden.

Shukovsky, thank God, paid no attention. He waited until I had sipped my drink. "Writers in America like bourbon?" he said.

"That sounds like the title of a post-modernist novel," I said.

No laughter from Shukovsky. "I am wrong?" he said.

I shook my head. "It's our kvass, tovarich," I said, like a toast.

He held up his glass, too. "When I was tovarich, nobody call me tovarich." He took more than a sip, and his laughter became more suave after that, more worldly sad for it.

"You here before?" I said, falling into his cadence.

He shook his head. "Milano, Paris..." He winked at me. "...Amsterdam."

"You like Flemish paintings, right?" I said.

"You...you..." He pointed a finger, but before he shook it, he decided to laugh instead.

Billie harrumphed. Then added, "I think you're talking about sex," and left us.

Shukovsky looked at her retreating ass and then quickly at the nearby guests who were hoping to insinuate themselves into our conversation. I gave them my dowager forbidding look. They saw I wanted them to scatter, and did.

In as near a whisper as he could project his voice, he asked me, "I get an agent? I do that?"

I scowled at my bourbon. "That's more difficult than finding a publisher," I said slowly, as intelligibly as I could. I knew this was a serious matter for the fellow and I did like him—a bit. He leaned forward; I knew no Mussorgsky would be forthcoming. Anyway, I preferred to talk shop with him than go home and feel the full force of my anxieties. "You need them," I said, and scowled some more.

"Yes?" Shukovsky said.

"You must never sign a contract..." I found myself stopping to mimic the action, "...without an agent. The publishers will skin you alive."

Shukovsky took a deep breath and then all the Scotch that was left in his glass. "I saw a publisher already." He held up three fingers.

"Three?" I said.

"Farrar and Straus and Giroux," he said, stumbling over each name.

This time it was I who laughed. No Mussorgsky, more like Gershwin. It started a shooting pain in my spine, the kind I had been attributing to—ha-ha—the back troubles we Americans suffer by the millions. I knew it was my DS now. The hell with cautions and warnings, I took the number 3: I wasn't going to drive a car.

My laughter stopped Billie, who was showing her dwarf groupie the kitchen so she could help out there. Shukovsky did not notice, but she pinched my right bun—punishment or caress?—and continued on. That gave me pause, as they say.

"No good?" Shukovsky said.

"No, no, very prestigious," I said as soberly as I could under the circumstances. "Very prestigious, indeed."

Billie turned back. "Who's prestigious?" she said, ready to fight. Or, anyway, play the leading role in any conversation.

"Your publisher," I said, and explained to Shukovsky, "They publish Billie."

"Yes," he said soberly, "Billie introduce me."

Aha, I thought, I guess she doesn't mind foreign competition. What was I doing here? I pressed my free hand at the small of my back and, in order to appear casual, looked around. For that matter, what was Shukovsky doing here? That settled it, I was going home. I tried to hand my glass to the pretty girl going by with an empty tray. Shukovsky intercepted it as he got up in response to Billie's sheep-dog maneuvers, and he drank it down without pause. He made a face. I felt sorry for him, but not enough to stay and make the trek to the New School with him like a good tovarich. Also, I still felt the pinch on my ass, and did not want to ponder what it signified.

Thom grabbed my arm when I reached out for the exit doorknob. “Now that we’ve been properly introduced,” he said, “can I ring your bell? There’s something I want to ask you.”

“Sure,” I said. “I gotta get out of here now.”

“I can’t wait, too,” Thom said, and quickly closed the door behind me after he whispered, “I won’t tell her you left. See you.”

I fled none too soon. I had the feeling that Thom was holding crowds back, his little body straining against the door, and after only a few paces I looked over my shoulder but no one was leaving Billie’s house. At Sixth Avenue, I was stopped by the light and again I looked back fearfully. Behind me, a block away, at Seventh Avenue, also waiting for the light, was a small group of people. My sight is not good anymore, but I was sure that at the head of it stood Billie, storming the barricades, this time without a drum. And, of course, not bare to the waist, flaunting youthful breasts.

I could see better ahead, across Sixth Avenue, and there on the corner stood Gwendolyn in a pose you see often in the Village: both her hands clasped behind Owen’s father’s neck, her face upturned with yearning and expectancy, her pelvis smack against his. She meant none of the endearments she had said to me. I made a quick left turn and headed for the A & P, a safe haven with its many aisles. I muttered to myself as I went along, “Help, help, somebody,” and became another of those demented New Yorkers hurrying along berating invisible demons.

Anxiety

The time has come for this Old Gent to come clean about everything that's wrong with him. In the realm of the physical, that is. There is nothing we Old Gents prefer more than to come upon another Old Gent and leisurely, savoringly exchange symptoms, blood-sugar and heart-pressure levels, medicines and dosages. We name each of our specialists as awesomely as if we were calling up the apostles of the New Testament. Our prescriptions are their epistles. Ah, what pleasure there is in all this. A stiff upper lip doesn't come naturally to any of us. Indeed, the real love relationship of an Old Gent may only occur, if he is sick enough, with another Old Gent, the sicker the better. We bond marxistically (this adverb is original with me) for our coming together is embedded in necessity: the best comradeship of all.

What better way to spend one's waning days than discussing the placid bladder nights that Hytrin brings—no shuffling anxiously to the john every fifteen minutes—to someone who knows the serenity this medicine bestows and is eager for you to finish your spiel to embark on his own experiences with Lopressor. Or to remind you that the onerousness caused by the deviling need to urinate lies less in shuffling through the apartment in the dark than in the superhuman effort it takes to sit up at the bed's edge and then rise to one's feet. No philosophizing goes on in these exchanges of the Old

Gents, only the particular merits of ibuprofen and acetaminophen and salicyclic acid. Ah, yes, I've had encounters with knowledgeable peers like these a few times, and I never once in our extended talks referred to literature, my real love.

Only last week, I spent the better part of an afternoon walking up and down Washington Square Park in pain hoping for a return bout with a retired subway conductor. When I met him on a bench one week earlier, he had been due to see his GP for his monthly checkup, and I was now determined to learn if his doctor had recalibrated his heart medicines and taken him off the diuretic as he had suggested he might. My search for him took place on a Thursday, the day of the week his daughter entertained three girlfriends, and if he was not in the park he might well be dead—he disliked those women so much, nothing could have kept him home. They were younger than he but nothing to look at, all at least fifty. He waved a hand forward to show they were way past their prime. He was an old Italian from Bleecker Street and he had married a girl from the neighborhood and started having children early. He was on the verge of achieving great-grandfatherhood. Not me, Fatso was Jewish and progressive, as we used to say, and in no hurry to raise kids.

I did not want him to be dead. He and the other Old Gent I talked to last week on the No. 5 for more than an hour, all the way to Washington Heights, were the only persons besides my doctors who knew I had prostate cancer. Actually, an enlarged prostate, I said no more than that. I gave the No. 5 guy my phone number, but he did not call. I didn't have his, because, would you believe it, he lived without a phone. He could not afford one, he said, and besides he did not like talking on the phone. He visited his son once a week, as he had done that day, and he preferred spending his money on cable and the Sports Channel which were both cheaper and less interfering. That was his word, interfering, and I liked it.

He was getting off at 168th Street, right near where I lived when I came to the city in 1937, but I planned to go on to Inwood for a last look at the Cloisters. By 155th Street we were such pals that he did not respond to my confession that the Spanish museum there was an old favorite of mine; he knew he did not have to be courteous anymore. Anyway, he probably had never spent time in it staring at the Duchess of Alba pointing to the name on the ground. His eyes gazed unacceptingly at Broadway rising ahead, and he said, "It's all the Dominican Republic now."

I said, "Watch out, I'm a Latino."

"Big deal," he said. "So am I. We're more liable to get diabetes."

"I have heard that," I said in Spanish, "but I have not accepted it."

He replied in American: "I was always a dirty holdout myself." Then gave in: "*¿Me entiendes*?"

In 1937, me and my aunt and uncle and cousins were the only people on 163rd Street who spoke Spanish. You could have said the same about most blocks in the neighborhood.

For the next ten blocks, the Old Gent repeated in genuine New York City American, "Lookit, will ya," like a Damon Runyon character.

When he got off, we shook hands. "Be careful, that's where they killed Malcolm X," I said.

"Here I come," he said lugubriously.

His mood clung to me the rest of the way. Because of him I composed the first poem I ever wrote as the bus lumbered up Fort Washington Avenue:

Roses are red,
Violets are blue.
He was always a Red
But oh so blue.

◇

I haven't come clean, have I? It's difficult: all of you out there exude health, if not well-being. You jog two miles a day through traffic, around the park, mowing me down on the sidewalks I frequent; you work out at the gym eying your muscles in *Chorus Line* mirrors; crowd the natural food stores for arcane foods. I am witness to all those proud pectorals, bulging calves, arcing thighs. I don't expect I can successfully woo you with illnesses, for that is what writers, even as loathsome as Celine, do, you know: woo, cajole, fawn, beg. Well, here goes.

Twice they have cleaved through my sternum, like any neighborhood butcher quartering a chicken for frying, to replace my aortic valve with a pig's. The second open-heart surgery became necessary when I forgot to take an antibiotic before keeping an appointment with my dentist. (The slightest nick in your gums can send a deadly virus straight to the implanted valve. There are many unfriendly germs in our mouths: there is nothing worse than our bites.) I was so eager to get away from Fatso that morning that I dashed out without the usual protection of two erythromycins in me. Fatso had a lunch date with two of her many old progressive friends turned feminist, and after the dentist's I decided to walk in Central Park (I lived in the Upper West Side then) and miss their equally deadly company. That sortie meant I also missed the erythromycin to be taken an hour or two after the dentist had fiddled with his pics and drills. Two days later, I awoke with the shakes.

Fever, of course. My jaws clacked open and shut at unstoppable speed, like dentures in animated cartoons. I let Fatso sleep on, and dialed Manuel's number. Not Randy's, for despite his exuberant, commanding presence, he breaks down in an emergency and needs help himself. Tony was already settled in the Hamptons and out of reach. Manuel lived directly across town, and had only to hear my crazy quavering voice to say, "Dad, I'll call your doctor and come straight over." He made it a couple of minutes before the ambulance arrived and at the very moment Fatso awoke and called for me to bring her, as obligation not favor, her morning cup of coffee. Manuel ordered her to remain in the apartment, and he stayed with me every minute until I was ensconced in a semi-private room at New York Hospital, the Eden that had on two other occasions provided me with the one sure refuge from Fatso: my paradisal aerie overlooking the East River. That morning, however, I could look at nothing.

I am taking too long with this endocarditis, but I love some of the stories connected with it and promise to be brief about other illnesses. I especially like the hallucinations. For two weeks it was touch and go with the endocarditis—apt name, right?—and during the first four days I also suffered unceasing hiccoughs. I remembered my impious cousin Pancho making fun, when I was a kid, of the pope dying hiccoughing, and would have laughed if the hiccough had allowed me. They were feeding me antibiotics intravenously. Without a stop, it seemed; powerful ones with ugly names that the anesthesia of the second operation has caused me to forget. The hours of deep sleep puncture a hole in your memory surrounding the times the operations took place—a sample of what Alzheimer's will be like. One of the few things I recall is Manuel and my Deere doctor—that's his name but I use it as an adjective, too—discussing the possibility of thorazine.

"Isn't that for schizophrenics?" Manuel said, out of the fund of psychiatric knowledge he acquired for his Jamesian novel about a classy nuthouse.

"It's been useful in some cases," the Deere boy said—sometimes I mean the adjective, sometimes I don't. This time I don't.

Nothing can make me forget the hallucinatory anxieties that followed my taking thorazine each night. An innocent enough looking capsule and, soon after nine, when visiting hours were over, my imagination took off. The first night I decided that the nurse was the owner of a bed and breakfast inn in rural Scotland. The house and outbuildings glowered and gleamed and were also scattered with earth tones—quite beautiful, I said to myself, but did not supply much distraction in the isolated countryside. Yet I also suspected we were in Hell's Kitchen, and now and then the noise of Times Square would be wafted into my little attic room. I accused her after breakfast of plotting to sell me hand-woven tweeds the colors of the old stone walls for an exorbitant price. A harmless dream, you might say, but it felt menacing. Still, I don't think I hiccoughed all of that first night, but I awakened with them.

The second thorazine night the head nurse for the floor came in while I was trying to remove the damn catheter inserted into my penis to extract my urine and empty it into a bag under my bed. "No, no, no," my private nurse said, "you're in no condition to be marching off to the toilet." She was a middle-aged English spinster, and she was subject to a personal modesty not usual with nurses: she drew the curtains round my bed to protect us from the sight of the two other curious patients in the room. Or vice versa. She could not, however, stop my talking, and I'm sure, in retrospect, everyone must have enjoyed my performance—wheedling, beseeching calls for her to take off the damn thing. I tried to pull it off myself and she intervened, and that is why, I dare say, the floor nurse showed up. Or was she merely making her rounds on first coming on duty?

She was young, beautiful, erect as a ballet dancer, and very likely half-Chinese. To me that accounted for the pronounced impassivity she displayed. Ancient silent-movie lore about Asians awakened in me. The thorazine had begun its work. These two foreigners were clearly a dangerous cabal: the pitiless beauty and her old crone of an imperialist partner. I sensed it was the head nurse I must fight. My Boxer Rebellion.

"Out!" I said. "You're trying to cover up what you are, but you don't fool me. I know, I know." She did not respond; she stared at me, daring me. "You have already sold out your own people—isn't that enough? Dragon lady! You're doing more of their dirty work. Out! You're not in charge—they are."

She left, and I went back to begging the imperialist crone for respite from the catheter, until the sleeping pill apparently took over. I awoke and she was gone. Randy and Manuel were looking at me. I hiccoughed: another enervating heart-stopping day ahead. One of them asked or was it both in unison?—"What happened, Dad?"

Why am I telling you all this? I'm going to cut out what followed, except to say that the two boys and my Deere doctor decided to switch me to a private room to spare the other patients, who when I looked their way, appeared more interested than upset, indeed stared as if I were the front page of the *New York Post*. But it turned out that the transfer could not happen until the next morning. I asked, "They expecting someone to die tonight?" Randy shook a finger at me—he liked that—but not Manuel. He knit his brows, as they describe that humorless look; he saves all his wit for his novels. The Deere boy took my pulse, and winked at me.

At that point none of us knew or suspected—except perhaps Randy—that my unmentionable behavior was a direct result of the thorazine. A good thing, too, or I should never have got rid of Fatso for the duration. Of my life, that is. Not that I did anything so terrible, but the thorazine kicked in early the next evening, while she sat on the one chair the hospital supplies per bed for visitors. The boys left when she arrived. The private nurse had taken off—on a coffee break, presumably, but I knew better. Fatso talked and I hiccoughed. She had not asked me how I felt—she never did—nor what the doctors said, and she had stared haughtily at the nurse when she tried to report to her. Fatso was extraordinarily able at emptying rooms, and it angered her that her victims did not remain in place. She was bored and my hiccoughs irked her, but she may have felt compensated by the fact that I could not escape.

My fit began creeping up on me—that was the distinction of thorazine, you could watch it approach, like a tide. But I held it back, fearing I was in for another bad night. Its eventual good consequences had not occurred to me. At home I usually made one cutting comment when I was angry with Fatso and then shut up. Or pretended I was on the phone to someone, telling anecdotes to a dead wire. Or several other ploys I had worked up over the years, thirty-nine long ones, to be exact. But then I saw that look of hauteur and thought of the opportunity at hand: I had the best excuse in the world, it was going to be different tonight.

"Bored?" I said with ill intent.

"It's no pleasure visiting here," she said. She had the ability I had always believed only Wasps could command of projecting her voice with such control that it was heard solely by the person she aimed it at.

I knew that if I responded angrily that everyone in the room would think I was the loutish sinner. Don't think she didn't know that; she manufactured a pleasant expression for her face to complete the picture, for anyone watching, of a long-suffering female. I tried smiling benignly, too.

"I'm so sorry," I said, knowing that sarcasm was lost on her.

She blinked, her way of accepting apologies, self-abnegations, tickets to the theater, whatever. "It's very boring at home, too," she said. "Nobody calls. You would think..." She shrugged and I waited for the zinger that was sure to follow. Another shrug and that meant she would dare anything. "Are they trying to tell me it's only you they are interested in? Well, maybe not the only one, but certainly you are number one. I wish they would not make it so obvious. It's scandalous. I don't see why I should entertain them in the future. You take them out somewhere—out of my sight."

I hiccoughed and was sorry I couldn't respond more suavely. "You think they could really like me more than you?" I said, and sneered.

But she was looking away and again missed the sarcasm.

"I have spent my life catering to your friends," she said. "But no more. It's the kind of male oppression everyone overlooks, the Chekovian boredom we have to bear."

That was it: I would not let this woman have Chekov.

"Don't pretend you are Fatso," I said, my voice getting stronger as I spoke. "Fatso knows nothing about Chekov." I raised my head from the pillow and yelled beyond her. "Hey, everybody, this is not Fatso! I don't have friends, only Fatso has friends. Call the police!"

"Shush," she said, and her voice turned into a dart. I lunged to one side and it went by me. "Shush," she added and launched another. What aim she had!—she almost got me the second time.

"Maybe she is Fatso!" I called out again, "A killer!" I made a pistol of the arm not tied to the IV. "Here goes. Boom, boom! I got her!"

She half-stood, looked around. I watched her hands. "Oh, oh," I heard her say. "Mercy, mercy."

"Fatso would never say that. You're a fake." Again, I appealed to the room. "They're after me." Fatso leans back on her ass and expects to be adored. She swings her legs out, but you still can't see her cunt. "Come and adore me, born the queen of the Upper West Side!"

I panted. I was scared but unintimidated. I wanted to run up and down the halls rousing the foot soldiers. I couldn't get away; I was tied to the place at one arm and my cock. I wiggled my toes—were my feet free? I fell back, opened an eye, she was in profile, calculating. Maybe she was Fatso? "I won't give you another baby, never," I said, testing her, and felt her hand pinching my big toe. Fatso had never touched a toe of mine. I heard a strange scurrying noise, opened both eyes this time and saw the curtain closing round my bed. It was moving on its own. Fatso was gone.

I did not know then that I had triumphed. I fell back into a hair-raising adventure with malevolent subway attendants insisting I pay twenty dollars per token. I was glued to the booth like a fly to flypaper, and strained to get away and could not. I called to the stream of Latinos hurrying through the station talking shrilly. None responded. Some backed all the way to the booth, not tc help me but instead to get sufficient impulse to jump the turnstiles. My voice could not get their attention; I could not send it out like a dart. I took a deep breath, gathering impulse myself, and called but only emitted a hiccough. I awoke. I have tried unsuccessfully since then to separate and analyze the mix of emotions churning in me that morning, but if someone had told me when I awoke that I would never see Fatso again, I should have felt better. Yes, indeed. Randy and Manuel were there again. Their eyes told me their mother had spoken to them. They humored me with tsk-tsk-tsk looks. With all his psychiatric medical lore, Manuel said, "Dad, I think it's the thorazine." Randy giggled, "No, she had it coming to her."

◈

Medicines, that is all I mean to talk about here. Thorazine had its way with me spectacularly, but I suspect that throughout the years others have sneaked up on me and deconstructed me. It is only thorazine, however, at which I can point an accusing finger. Let me just list the ones I have taken. During this stay at the hospital with endocarditis, they fed me strong antibiotics, but I cannot name them. I never remember the names of intravenous antibiotics, because they hang up there beyond an old man's vision instead of snuggling in a little plastic phial you hold in your hand and study. After my first open-heart surgery came the deluge of medicines. Until then I took an occasional aspirin. But now I took Lanoxin (to strengthen and steady my heartbeat) and Furosemide (a diuretic useful with high blood pressure) and Lopressor (a stronger medicine, also for high blood pressure) and two shots daily of insulin for you know what. And of course for three months following each operation, Coumarin, a blood thinner which is more popularly used to poison rats, causing them to hemorrhage to death; they did not want any blood clots floating around in my body from the many transfusions during each procedure.

See how knowledgeable I have become—I say procedure instead of operation!

A sense of incompletion made me look at the medicine cabinet after writing the above, and, sure enough, I discovered I had not listed one more medicine—Zestril. I don't quite know what it is indicated for. I am not so knowledgeable after all.

After two weeks of endocarditis and heavy antibiotics, my old valve had to be replaced. It was as much of a wreck as I. They checked this deterioration with a catherization—my second. I am not going to describe it; I leave you to find out about that on your own. After the second procedure (ha-ha!) to replace the aortic valve, I got a fungus infection in the incision down the middle of my chest. For three months I took Cipro once a day ($5) and an anti-fungal whose name I cannot remember, most likely because each capsule cost $13. I also—though this part does not strictly qualify as a medicine—had to remove the bandages covering the suppuration and clean the area with Sodium Chloride Irrigation USP, a bottled liquid that looked like plain water to me. Then without much enthusiasm I taped on new bandages. I engaged in this revolting job at least twice daily, and although a new tape had been invented that did not leave you raw when removed, I did shave gingerly some days around the wound as self-protection.

It is rather difficult for other old geezers to top these all-star ailments. Especially when I add to them the cellulitis and the epididymitis; this last a gratuitous inflammation of the testicles which was not caused by any diverting antics. Both of them also required intravenous antibiotics and a stay at the hospital, not so much fun now that it was not a refuge. With Fatso gone, I was already living in my favorite zone, the Village. The sensational view of the East River and the funicular to Roosevelt Island became boring after one day, but I did get a lot of reading done. This latter expression is one I don't much care for. Since my Tampa childhood, reading has never been a duty or a chore, not only a delight but a way of talking to people much less disappointing than those you come across from day to day.

There—I have looked back at the years following the first operation solely to recall the medicines I have taken (there is something of the pedant about me), although there was a certain excitement about that first surgery: I felt like a pioneer. It occurs to me that since then I have never gotten the flu or even a cold as rampant as the ones in television commercials. Maybe a day-long sore throat, but no more than that. Just as in the same years I have—with the disappearance of Fatso to the Vermont house—cut down on irksome day-to-day relationships. So: no superficial illnesses or friends; open-heart procedures instead, and love, the worst catastrophe of all.

◇

The next knock on my door I could scarcely manage the lock: my darling had come to say goodbye. Tomorrow she was leaving. It was Thursday noon, I had already taken ibuprofen and a number 3 with its load of codeine and Tylenol. My little place resounded with a Bartok sonata, as turbulent as me, and Youri Egorov hit a resounding chord as I opened the door. It was Thom.

"That's all right," he said. "I'll go away."

"What?" I said, and tried not to look down the hall, if only because I felt I might pitch forward.

He placed a hand on his forehead and then slapped it; it was very expressive. "You were expecting someone else."

I lied by shaking my head. "Come in," I said.

He brought his hand down, but he did not step forward. "I forgot what my excuse was," he said.

"That's okay," I said, and I stepped back to let him in and lost my balance. I reached for the wall, but I missed it. How could that be?

I did not see Thom come into my little hallway, but he did not let me fall. He pushed up against me and held both arms around my middle with more strength than I thought his little body could gather.

I said, "I'm all right."

"No, you're not," he replied, and kept one arm around my waist and with the other closed the apartment door. "You're pale, too."

I took a deep breath, then shook my head; I didn't quite know what I meant.

He kept looking up into my face. "You think we can walk right there to the chair?"

"Sure," I said.

Not since Abuelo, my Cuban grandfather, died has anyone firmly grasped my elbow and thus helped me navigate the space ahead. Of course, I was nineteen or so when Abuelo last guided me across the street. Thom did very much the same thing, but although I was humoring him, I did need steadying. He was a good boy.

"There you go," he said when I was down all the way in the wing chair. "How about something to drink?" he suggested.

I said, "I would like a real drink. Wouldn't you?"

"Not a good idea," he said.

I agreed.

"Tea, then," he said. "Though my grandfather used to say, 'Nothing like a snort.'"

"Used?" I said.

"He got hit by a car," Thom said.

I liked that. Putting a real distance between that death and my condition. No comparison, he was saying.

A really thoughtful response. I patted the hand still leaning on the arm of my chair.

"I'm making us both tea," he said, and stepped right into the kitchen before I could stop him. Not that it was far away—not like the grand places my sons live in. He called back, "I can figure it out."

"My grandfather also got hit by a car," I said to myself. I was alone and facing away from the kitchen, so I touched my heart—which is about as spiritual as I get—and added, "Abuelo."

Thom stuck his head out of the kitchen. "I know a little Spanish and I got very good hearing," he said. When he came out with the tea—he had even found a tray—he added, "Did you like your grandfather, too?"

I nodded and even considered telling him about Abuelo, but it was at this moment that he told me his name and about not being one of *the* Abercrombies. He served me the tea like a professional. When I nodded to his adding milk, he said, "It figures—everyone west of the Volga or whatever."

The very first swallow made me feel better. "You did that like a professional," I said as thank-you.

"I am," he said, and smiled, a joke he kept to himself. "In the theater, before you make it, you got to do whatever for a living." He sipped and he, too, liked the tea. "Not bad. People used to scorn tea balls, so uncouth when they first appeared..." He broke off and rattled his cup, laughing. "Hey, that sounds x-rated! Tea balls!"

"Volga," I said, feeling like a teenager. In my head, that is.

He was quick with his comeback: "You're Ole Man River."

We laughed like a couple of kids, then I said, "That's for sure," and made a deprecating gesture.

"What?" he said, apprehensively.

"And I just dribble along."

"Hey...I'm on the banks of the Wabash myself." He changed to an intent look; he wanted to be taken seriously. "I think to be...I mean, being older is the best thing you can be."

"Thank you," I said, "but I can think of a couple of other things myself."

His mouth was half open. He seemed ready to confess, to argue, to volunteer heartfelt demurrers, but he decided against it. He put his cup on the floor, asked, "How are you feeling now?" and half stood to obey any orders. "Dad?"

I lied. "Well. Thank you for the tea; it perked me up." But I kept my hands firmly on the chair arms.

He looked into my eyes, questioning what he saw. I did not understand: I couldn't look that ill.

"Or I can call you Pop, if you prefer."

I said, "Now, that cannot be your reason for ringing my bell..."

And it rang. Rather, there was a knock. This time it must be Gwendolyn. I was not nervous anymore, but Thom seemed sprung from a cage.

"I'll get that," he said, and I saw how quickly he moved, how lithe he was, and I thought that I must have been like that, too. Had I?

"Sweetheart..." Gwendolyn began and stopped when she faced Thom.

I could look into the little hallway. She executed gestures of surprise. She waved at me, she nodded at Thom, also with some surprise, but she did not make a move to come in.

Thom half-turned. "*That*'s what I wanted to tell you: she's leaving. For L.A., not for good and..." He stepped back and said no more. To Gwendolyn: "Sorry, I didn't mean to hog the conversation."

Gwendolyn smiled and shook her head and made another of her darling gestures. "Don't let me interrupt," she said, and took one tiny step back.

"Come on," Thom said.

I did not know the two were close or even acquainted other than as floor neighbors, but of course youth goes to youth. And while I was at it, I should tell her it was okay to embrace her husband or the father of her child on Sixth Avenue. I had the nerve but not the inclination.

I waved her in. "Have some tea—Thom will make it."

"Thank you," she said, and closed the door behind her. "I'll make it."

Thom shook his head. "It's my job..."

She stood in the doorway to the kitchen. It was a stand-off. A short one. He gave up. "You only gotta pour hot water on a tea ball," he said. "It's all there on the counter." He came inside, picked up his cup from the floor and sat across from me again. "Actually, you look better."

"Thanks to you," I said.

He was hopeful that Gwendolyn heard me. How did I know? One does, that's all.

"Nothing wrong with you," he said. "Just a little passing dizziness. Ah, me, you could say that about me all the time."

Gwendolyn returned, holding her cup like Liza Doolittle at her first upper-class tea. "Who was dizzy?" she asked.

I knew she knew, but Thom tried to change the subject. "More like ditsy, that's me."

She took one of the two ladder-backs at the New England drop-leaf dining table and placed it facing me, sideways to Thom. Why was she miffed with Thom? Because he had hurried to announce her LA trip? She arranged her long, old-fashioned granny dress so that it fell evenly to the floor and rested her cup and saucer on her knee. What a beautiful girl she is. I shook my head over the feelings of forgiveness that flooded me. If she only knew...

She did not reply to Thom or look his way, but she took a beat and it told him to stop. There was a vein of iron in her. He got up as if to leave, and I perversely winked at him to keep him there: I was repaying her for kissing her fellow on Sixth Avenue.

"How are you?" she said to me, giving that old greeting a new earnest reading. She still let her head lean towards her right shoulder to show sincerity, but there was a motherly air about her now. How had that leap been executed?

"You leave tomorrow," I said. "You must be excited."

"Are you really all right?" she insisted. "Randy worries about you."

"Randy?" I said. Thom looked curious and I added for his sake: "My son?"

She wished him out of the apartment. I could tell that. I could tell everything about her. Love does that. Maybe she could tell about me, too, for she greeted Thom directly for the first time. A mere, "Oh, hello, Thom," as if to say scat.

I said, "When did you talk to Randy?"

"Oh..." she said as if her talking to Randy were so unimportant or so usual that it scarcely mattered.

"Would you do me a favor?" I spoke to Thom, my way of rebuking her and telling him to stay. I pointed to the stereo playing a Haydn trio. "Would you turn that off?"

He enjoyed doing that, and the silence made my earlier question about Randy more pointed. I said to her, "I'm sorry, you were saying..."

There was nothing in her manner that showed she was aware that I was countermanding her unspoken directive to Thom. To leave, that is. (God, I sound like Henry James.) Nor did she appear to take in that there was any particular point to my question about Randy. (I promise, no more involutions.) In fact, she seemed to have forgotten what we were talking about altogether.

"Randy," I said, and held my voice steady to show I expected an answer.

"Oh, you didn't know?" she said brightly. "Randy may be out in L.A. and he wanted our number there in case—isn't that wonderful! He knows so many people. Actually, he thinks that Stacey..."

"Who?" I said.

Thom filled me in. "Owen's father."

Gwendolyn took two beats this time.

"Randy thinks there is a student film they start shooting next week that...wasn't it you who recommended us to Randy? It's darling of you, it really is."

I didn't mean to take a beat myself, but it soon became too late for me to disclaim credit. She reached out and took my hand. "You *are* feeling all right. He worries, you know, that's why he called...to see if I had observed anything unusual..."

She placed her right hand on her forehead, palm out, that gesture that goes right to my heart. "Oh, oh, oh!" she trilled. "He told me specifically not to tell you, and here I've blurted it out."

"Tell me what?" I said, at sea.

"He says you're a curmudgeon and you won't have it," she said. "Now, why would he say that? I told him he's wrong—you're sweetness itself. Why would you be angry to learn that your dear son—your sons!—he talked to the others..."

"What! What!" I said.

"You would like it that they're concerned, I assured him," she said, and held out her cup to Thom to take away so that she could gesture unrestrainedly. "I know for certain now that Randy is very concerned. You would want them all to gather round, to help, to just be there."

I said, "That's the way it is with you Irish. Taking off with the ball before they've put up the goal posts."

That was a standard denunciation of mine, but she had won me over and it sounded less harsh than usual—indeed, complimentary. Anyway, I was ready to buy anything she wanted to sell: everybody loves me, okay, everybody loves me. "There's nothing wrong with me," I added, nevertheless. "I don't need any help."

Thom winked at me to show my dizziness was our secret.

"He asked me to keep an eye on you—isn't that sweet?—but of course I leave tomorrow." She looked around and unaccountably smiled at Thom. "But if Stacey stays, then...and if not, I told him, we have a friend..." She broke off to wave Thom towards her. "Right next door to you...right?'

"Right!" Thom said. He was won over, too.

Too—do I need to underline it? Was he another rival? The hell with all suspicions! I must have looked very happy, for my darling Gwendolyn leapt up and impulsively threw her arms around my shoulders and kissed me on each cheek. She drew back her head and gazed deeply into my eyes and quickly pecked me on the lips. Hers were soft and giving. Thank God, I shaved in the morning, I said to myself, and felt my heart thumping away. Thom came into focus; he was looking down at the tea cup on the floor. I guess he was embarrassed. He pulled himself out of it. "I will," he said. "I'll take care of you. That's what I came to tell you." The three of us laughed as one—the last time I was at peace with the world.

"Off to L.A., then!" she announced, hugged me again, and dragged Thom away with her.

◇

Of course, Randy got Stacey the role in his student's movie. I heard about that when they rang my bell the next morning, and by then I was psychologically ready for Gwendolyn's departure, or a number 3 had helped persuade me. I was up and down, back and forth all night despite two ambiens: love and paranoia are stronger than chemicals. She was leaving now, not in the afternoon, as I had thought, hoping by then to have reached a state of indifference to it all.

Thom carried her bag to the elevator. Stacey held Owen in his arms, and the kid was so stupid he was smiling and waving goodbye. His mother would be unencumbered in L.A.—I should have foreseen that yesterday, but I was stupid, too. Randy was not there or we should have made up the whole dramatis personae and the 1920's hallway our thrust stage. Gwendolyn spread out her arms as if taking a curtain call that thanked the whole house.

I learned everything from them there and then, not from Randy. He had not called me, but he had apparently been on the phone with them throughout the late afternoon and evening. As soon as Gwendolyn with her stops and starts and by-the-ways let me know the facts (which I see now has taken me hours to reconstitute into significant order), Stacey walked towards me with a huge romantic lead's smile, one muscular arm holding up Owen and the other stretched out offering a handshake. He wore only a pair of jeans and nothing else, not even on his manly feet. "I know you, I know you, I feel it," he said, and I saw he had perfect teeth. "The name's Stacey Grundig."

What chance did Randy and I have with him for a rival? How did we even get a foot in the door?

Why did I always ask myself questions to which I knew the answers? Or part of the answer. I still did not know why the darling girl had initially turned to me. Love? Paternal warmth? I locked into the kind of stasis that old folks fall into, from an excess of thoughts, not, as quick younger people think, because their gears need oiling.

She had cajoled her huge bag into the elevator before any of us thought to help her, much as she always maneuvered Owen and his stroller without expecting a hand. Thom pulled back the elevator's outer door to keep her there a moment. "So long, sweetie, don't worry about a thing," he said. She waved at him as if she were in a moving car. For a split second her face looked sad, an unplanned unactorish reaction. From behind him, I smiled and nodded and I think she caught that and consequently grinned as the inner door wiped across my view and whisked her away. Thom leaned a hand on the elevator door, and Owen stopped waving and looked nonplussed. Stacey winked at me as if that were a large statement. Perhaps it was.

I said, "Is a car coming for her?"

Thom ran for the stairs. "I'm gonna help her!" he yelled, and he was so light and agile we could not hear him taking the steps.

"Pop, come in and have a cup of coffee with us," Stacey said. "You don't mind my calling you Pop, do you?

I talked to Randy on the phone last night and this morning and so..." He chuckled so beautifully it was like a Verdi recitative. "What can I say, I feel like a member of the family."

I think it was the sad look on Gwendolyn's face—of short but keen duration—that left me malleable. I obediently followed him the few paces to their apartment. He courteously held the door open for me, and only after I passed through went inside himself. "I think I'll leave it open," he said, and pushed a toy against it as a doorstop. "So Thom will look-see and join us."

This was my first time beyond the door jamb: Jesus entering Jerusalem on Palm Sunday. It was much more than a half century since my one summer's short stay in Methodism, but I knew what lay ahead in that venue—spiritually and physically. Joy now, mortal suffering later. I had other less metaphorical sources of knowledge—my early years with Fatso—and I came down to earth quickly. With my first inhalation I identified that baby odor that cannot be scrubbed away. I was not surprised either that Stacey had to remove a moist towel from the back of the easy chair to which he pointed me. On my own, I side-stepped the strewn toys.

But I was surprised that Stacey should be aware of any of this. "The bedroom's a total disaster," he said with complacency, "but it's pretty much broken-field running all over the place."

"There were three in my house," I said.

Stacey didn't get it.

I added, "Two other boys besides Randy."

He put Owen down and said, "This character has a special talent." He tried to act nonchalant, but I saw that he checked on Owen's progress to the bedroom by cocking his head while he stood in the kitchen doorway. "The coffee's ready...milk and sugar?"

"We used to put them in a playpen," I said, "and throw them some hay once in a while."

Stacey listened politely, and said, "Playpens are a no-no now, I forget why," and emitted his musical laugh.

No use wasting my wit on him. "Milk and sugar," I said.

The moment he went inside I asked myself, why did I mention Randy? He'll bring him up soon enough. I was also thinking—actually, deciding; I rush to conclusions—that his manufactured laugh showed he was, unlike Gwendolyn, an actor in the old tradition, all surfaces and putty and tics. Actually, I prefer them—or used to, rather, in the days I inveighed against the mumblers—but I can and do sling that Actors Studio lingo now with the best of them. Art, art, you can talk forever about art, even theater art, although with me it's at least *er* not *re*. I could hear Stacey talking to me from the kitchen, being a good host, and saw Owen come to the door of the bedroom and stare at the Old Gent. I did not go in for any kitchy-koo stuff, so he went back into the bedroom. Hadn't Gwendolyn worked up all her performances with me strictly from the outside? No, yes—I must decide. Never was esthetics so important.

Here I was, in the sanctuary of my Irish lass, and despite the debris, my eyes went straight to the copy of *Jack* on the coffee table, rather, the foot locker that passed for one. On it were the breakfast remains... orange juice glasses, mugs, a bowl with soggy corn flakes at the bottom, a butter dish with melted traces. There were also two rolled-up pairs of socks, the *New York Times* of two days ago and *Backstage*. A postcard stuck out from *Jack*. With an eye out for Stacey's return, I removed the dirty glass from atop it and took the book in my hands. The card marked the beginning of the second chapter called "*Jack Buys His First Over-the-Counter Stocks*"—she had probably read no further. The card's front showed a dreamy photo of a theater in San Diego. The other side contained, along with her name and address, the greeting: "Love ya, Buddy." Are modern actors like Gwendolyn so aesthetically wedded to truth, capable of duplicity?

It seemed important that Gwendolyn and I had never discussed Brecht's theater of alienation. Would she stand outside the character and indicate (ah, that's such a terrible verb in Method acting) to the audience how they should feel about a character, to remind them relentlessly that she is an actor and not the character whom they must judge and not be one with? Would I hang a crude sign on the proscenium—or anywhere near the audience in what they now call the playing area—to proclaim where the scene is taking place or, indeed, what is taking place? I might, but Gwendolyn never. Still, hadn't the darling worked up all her performances with me strictly from the outside? If not, ah, then...happiness loomed. It meant that she would not, could not fake any response. I must get out of here and savor this possibility, my salvation.

Stacey appeared before me extending a coffee mug, and as if he knew what I was thinking, plunged right in: "Poor Gwennie, it's an audition factory out there and that's the worst thing in the world for actors like us," he said. "When you know how long it takes to get inside a character, it's like being nailed to the cross. Here's the script—start reading!"

He tapped me on the knee for emphasis and turned on his bare heels before I could clear my throat, looked in at Owen in the bedroom, dashed into the kitchen and emerged with a mug for himself. He leaned his tight buttocks into the edge of a futon couch and looked at me earnestly. "That's why I admire your son Randy. He didn't put me through that kind of hell. I really appreciate that."

Beggars can't be choosers and that's what Randy is, I thought but did not think it polite to say. I could have been wrong, anyway: acting is the only profession whose members are eager to work for nothing—at first. I merely nodded, and I am sure he thought my pride in Randy ran too deep for casual comment. Did he suspect, as I did, that Randy was merely getting him out of the way? Actually, I was in agony trying to absorb the morning's news and the postcard from Buddy. I should be home for another reason: to see if Randy would have the nerve to call me and explain all these new shenanigans. His ingenuity would be, as they say, taxed.

There must have been a pause, for Stacey's voice when it again got through my fog sounded real, poignant and unsure. "Pop, am I going to lose Gwennie to?..."

The shock was too great for me to stop him or answer his question. Randy had fooled no one. I had but that one thought in mind and fell into a real old man's stasis this time.

Stacey looked down and lowered his voice. "To you," he finished, and it was no longer a query.

Thank God, he was fooling. What a relief. I could not manage a smile so soon, however, but his own expression did not change. I was wrong; he looked very serious. He sat so close to me that he only had to move slightly, soundlessly to fall on his knees before me. He stretched his free hand upward and brought my face to his and rubbed it against mine, first on one side, then the other. He breathed audibly through his lips.

"Wait!" I finally said.

Later, I asked myself what I meant by that, but I did not do so at the moment because things happened so rapidly, as they say in fiction.

For one thing, Thom came in.

Another: Stacey kept his hand around my nape. He glanced up at Thom, took a beat and then planted a light Jesus-kiss on my forehead. I can say that the look on his face was unaffected by Thom's entrance. As for me, I had not fainted and was as alert as a writer needs to be. "We'll talk some more about this," Stacey said, and rose to his feet without any of his joints creaking.

Various matters warred in my old head. Was Stacey beseeching me to relinquish my hold on the dear girl? Then she really was sincere with me! And what did Thom think of this crazy scene? Should I be embarrassed? He had without warning come upon Stacey embracing me, and he must be as stunned, I supposed, as some bewildered passing nomad who ran into the crowd nailing Jesus to the cross. This terrible simile is a sign of the megalomanical egocentricity I have to watch out for in myself, a kind of job-related hazard. There I was, getting into the act with the lord so many people worship and entertaining the notion that anyone could think there was an element of eroticism in Stacey's hug. This last was not megalomania but the madness of old age, obviously, for I was always a sexist, no doubt, but not a macho on the alert, like Hemingway, for threats to his masculinity, whatever that is.

All this was too much for me to hold in my head at once. Later, later, I said to myself, I must get home and think, think, and take a number 3.

Thom said to Stacey, "I'm glad you didn't let Gwen see how upset you are," and added, before Stacey could respond, "Where's Owen?"

Stacey heard no sarcasm in Thom's statement. It had not occurred to him until then that sorrow at his wife's departure should have been his primary emotion, and he made a gesture of both acceptance and apology as if Thom were directing him in a scene. He nodded for good measure: he'd "keep" that for next time, as they say in their milieu.

Thom said, "Well, she's off," and I saw that he was truly sorry.

"There's lots of coffee," Stacey said, and pointed to the kitchen. "Get yourself some. I just looked in on Owen."

But Thom looked into the bedroom, anyway. He did not go to the kitchen for coffee, but came over to me, cutting Stacey off. "You're all right?" he said, stroked my shoulder with one hand in the kind of comforting gesture you see at funerals, and kept his back to Stacey. "You're going to miss her, Dad."

It took an effort but I got to my feet. "Actually, I don't see Gwendolyn as much as all that," I said coolly, and then found a spot on the coffee table where I could insinuate the mug I had been holding. "Excuse me, gentlemen, but I've got a few things I must do."

"Oh," said Stacey, "I did hope..." He held one hand over his bare left pectoral and looked yearningly. "I'll see you soon, Pop."

"Pop?" Thom said.

He came alongside me as if meaning to see me to my apartment. "No need," I said, and nodded and smiled politely. "I know my way."

◇

In fact, I just made it. I leaned back against my door after I closed it, like an overwrought heroine in an old movie. The phone rang. Or had it been ringing all along? I had no heart for it. I commanded it to stop. It did, before the answering machine could take over. It must be some miser, saving on local calls. Randy, very likely. If this were fiction, that's what I would invent: have Randy, a very different Randy, call to announce to an unsuspected rival—his old father!—that he is in love with Gwendolyn.

I went into the kitchen, poured seltzer in a small glass, sang badly *Mein water*! *Mein water*!, and heard the phone start up again. I gave up that turbulent *lied* and tried another: *Wie im Morgenglanze*... But Schubert's mellifluousness always escapes me. Anyway, it had no effect on the phone. I wanted to sit at my desk in peace and ponder whether one number 3 would be enough.

"Stop it," I said loudly, and again it did.

I finally reached my desk in what is nominally the bedroom, adjusted the pillows on the back and seat of my swivel chair, and straightened my back. The last always makes me feel purposeful. There were eleven plastic bottles in the upper right-hand corner bunched together in front of the Mont Blanc inks, of which there are four; I use different color inks to impel me to write on low-energy days. All these add up to fifteen bottles. On top of the shortwave radio (to which I never really listen) sat four bottles of vitamins (which I never take). There was still plenty of room for my various notebooks, the old mug filled with pens, the two-volume edition of the OED and the phone and its answering machine; but it requires determination to dust the top of this desk. I decided on three Extra Strength Tylenol.

I swung in my chair and looked at the two walls of books in order not to think. The wall across the room contained a shelf of books that for many years I have meant to give a second break: *Moby Dick*, Goethe's *Faust* and *The Sorrows of Wether*, *The Complete Works of William Shakespeare*, a couple of George Eliots, etc. It amuses me to have them there, to suffer my snubs when

I am in a bad mood. I looked at them now, malevolently. Bores. The phone rang, and with my back to it up close its sound buzzed through me as if I were being electrocuted.

I flung up an arm, one of the few acts I could still execute without effort, and pointed at *Faust*. "Mephistopheles, I am ready for a pact with you!" I sang out.

The phone stopped.

"Hey," I said. I pointed to Goethe again. "Is it a deal?"

That bit of Walt Disney humor did not assuage my suffering. Nor did all my busyness at the desk keep Gwendolyn at bay in my mind. A misogynist should not fall in love.

The phone rang once more and this time I picked it up.

It was you know who. "Say, Dad, I've been ringing you. Weren't you there? Did you hear my ring?"

"Why didn't you leave a message?" I said.

"I'm calling from home," he said, and then paused.

"And you didn't want to be overheard," I said. "Or you didn't want to waste any local calls?"

Ashamed to confess to one of those motives or both, he went right into his song and dance. "Dad, I was able to do a favor for your young friends. I suggested the fella for a role in one of..."

"I know all about that," I said. "The fella's name, by the way, is Stacey Grundig."

Randy never feels a rebuke if there is any indirection in it: a brick wall does have to fall on him. And then he's not even bruised.

"Well, I'm actually calling to tell you I'm taking a late plane for L.A.," he said.

I waited.

"Aren't you surprised?" he said. "The Dean's been after me to sign up a couple of names—a has-been director, an editor, or maybe some star passing through to do puff lectures for free, you know, for next term, and I did..."

"I know all about that, too," I said.

"But my real reason for going is that right after I saw you, I went to my office and there was a message from Dawn Ippolito..."

"Who's she?" I asked hopefully. Another mistress? His real reason for going to L.A?

"Dawn Ippolito is Riverview Studios," he said in a tone usually reserved for the retarded, "and saw that memoir article of mine on the Panther trial—remember? She wants to talk to me about it. Isn't that interesting!"

My head started swimming again. "What memoir?"

"Actually, it was a book review I did for the *Nation*," he said. "I had to defend the Sixties from these slime deconstructionists."

"What does this all have to do with your going to Hollywood?" I asked. I don't know why I asked, except that I believe in lucidness. "I think I have to hang up."

"Dad, wait, are you all right?" he said urgently.

"Yes, I am," I said with more energy than I could spare. "Or I will be when I straighten your messages out. You're going to Hollywood about a book review?"

"Shawn wants me to have lunch tomorrow," he said, and made his voice airy to show he was aping her. "Let's lunch tomorrow and mull over a few things."

I had to pursue it. "What things?"

"What with Spike Lee and Malcom," he explained, "black revolutionaries are very hot right now."

"Forget it; it's okay with me," I said, giving up. He would never come right out about Gwendolyn. "Spike Lee is black," I added, unable to be nice to him.

"Well, I could end up doing a script for her, Dad," he explained patiently, "or at least being a consultant on the project."

And meanwhile he could also cash in one of the two plane tickets and pocket it. "I see. I have to hang up," I said. "Goodbye."8

Again, I said to myself, a misogynist should not fall in love.

"Papi!" It was so loud and sharp a call for Randy that I did not hang up. "You there?"

I made a noise.

"Actually, there's something else I want to talk to you about—Dr. Deere?"

"What's the matter with him?" I was alerted. "Or with you—don't you have your own doctor?"

"I'm all right," he said, but he was reluctant to give up an opportunity to complain. (A fatso gene.) "My lower back is threatening to go out of line again."

"You know what that's from, don't you?" I said.

"Papi," he said, "don't embarrass me."

"Okay, goodbye," I said.

"Wait!" he said, not as loud this time. "I called Dr. Deere. I've been meaning to do so for the last couple of weeks. I worry..."

"Gwendolyn Costello tells me you worry about me," I said. "Who else is your confidante? No—don't answer that. I don't have time, I'm hanging up."

I hung up with enough energy left over to propel me out of the chair. I went over to the bores and thought it might help if I read one of Shakespeare's fake love-anguish sonnets, even if they are all conceits and none deeply felt. The volume of his complete works is a big one—all those deadly plays!—and I jiggled the shelf when I pulled it out. The shelf is a moveable one, and the toggles at one end gave. The books slid down that side, but only one fell to the floor. Goethe's *Faust*. It broke into three pieces.

I explain this in detail because I do not believe in the supernatural or in Scottish witches, like Shakespeare. I do not want anyone to think it was an omen or an augury or a divination. The book was a brittle ancient Everyman edition bought during my first year in New York City for nineteen cents, in the years before sales taxes, at a department store that no longer exists. Its glue must have turned into fragile crystal.

Still, I played it like high drama. "*No, no*!" I gasped throatily, like Don Giovanni to the Commendatore who is trying to drag him down to death and hell.

The sound of my defiance still echoed in the room when, again, the phone rang. I stepped on *Faust* to get to my desk. "Go to L.A.," I growled into the phone.

"Not on your life," was the reply. It was a deep voice, but not Randy's. It was Billie Gladiola, but I had no room left for surprise. "Who're you consigning to hell?"

"I'm sorry, Billie," I said. "I was talking to myself."

"Better than to Shukovsky," she said.

Again, I said I was sorry.

There was a pause while, I'm sure, she snapped her gum. "Actually, I don't blame you for chickening out," she said. "Literature and socialism are the last things on his mind."

"Hmmm," I went.

"And to tell the truth, on mine, too, old comrade," she said. "I'm throwing in the towel—I was never very good on pride and all that—and calling a male."

Confused, I said, "You're calling a male—a man?"

She laughed her short hard laugh. "You're just like me," she said. "You've forgotten how to go about the old mating game, if we ever knew it."

"I'm the male?" I said. Truthfully, I was surprised.

"Why not?" she said.

Jesus, I thought. "Why do you wanna ruin a perfectly good relationship?"

"You promise not to tell anybody?" she said. Her pause was just for effect. I knew I wasn't to say anything, and I didn't want to. Females are too risky when they are on the prowl.

She changed her shtick and waited me out. I said, "Okay, I promise."

"I love cop movies," she said, "and I no longer have anybody to take me. You can't go to these things alone." Another pause for effect while we both were supposed to be mourning her husband's passing. "All my lady friends are opposed to violence in films—and I am, too, officially."

Should I laugh sympathetically? I temporized, "I have forgotten what my stand is on that issue."

"There's a new Clint Eastwood," she said.

I could hear she thought she had sunk pretty low.

I was still wary. "Isn't he a Republican?"

"Shush," she said. "Bite your tongue."

"Just the movie?" I said. "No demonstration."

I had gone too far. "Listen," she began, and I could tell she was throwing caution to the winds, as well as me. "You can go..."

At this point, an extraordinary thing happened. The operator came on. "Sir, sir," she said. "There is an emergency call for you. If you'll hang up, they can get through."

"What!" Billie barked. "What's this, Gerry!"

My darling Gwendolyn! I did not think to say anything to Billie; I hung up with a slam. Gwendolyn must still be at Kennedy. I stared at the phone and wished it to ring. And it did, of course, and of course it was Randy.

"Papi, what is wrong?" he said. "Is it your health?"

"You're going to L.A. to screw Gwendolyn Costello," I said. "You're turning me into your pimp, that's what's wrong."

He replied in a hurt, hushed voice. "Don't say that, Papi. You know I take my relationships very seriously."

It occurred to me that it might not have been he who persuaded the operator to get on my line. "Just a moment," I said. "Did you speak to the operator?"

"I've been very worried," he said. "You have been quite hostile lately—it may be a symptom. You see, don't you?"

"Did you or didn't you?" I demanded.

"It's not as if I came on your conversation and eavesdropped," he said, sounding like the most reasonable of human beings. "She merely told me that she would let you know you had an important call..."

"It's no use," I said. "What do you think there's to eavesdrop about?"

He paused just a moment. "That's what I want to know."

"Nothing," I said.

"That's all I wanted to hear," he said, and exhaled as if a burden had been lifted. "Now I can go to L.A. with a clear conscience."

I began to protest his line of questioning by saying, "It's an invasion of my privacy," but this liberal cliché made me chuckle and I became tolerant. It occurred to me that by doing so he had, in fact, saved me from Billie Gladiola. I should also learn to trust my sweet Irish lass and stop imagining that every man who comes near her has a chance.

"Okay, have a good time," I said, but could not let him off entirely (he had had the nerve to interfere with my phone line) and added, "I suppose that's something one doesn't have to urge on you."

"I'll be back in two days," he said, winding up. "I want to talk to you then about a really thorough checkup."

"Sure," I said automatically. It sounded sarcastic and I was glad. It must have been the example of Fatso's couch-potato immobility that turned Randy into an indefatigable busybody. I thought of a final stinger: "You'll need it the way you're running around."

I hung up and thought: I, the least technological of persons, lead a life ruled by the telephone and word processor. They are the pillars of my house and existence. To have an operator break in, as just happened for the first time in my life, upset the serenity of my world. Indeed, I am led by the nose by these mechanisms. They are a mystery to me, and any departure from their grooved performances dislocates me. I understand neither of them the way I intuitively understand, say, the planting and care of a vegetable garden. I kept one in Vermont which I started from scratch—spading up the sod, shaking out the good soil caught in its roots, etc.—and I always thought I did it well because I inherited a propensity for it from my Galician peasant forefathers. A fruitful line of thought that—does technology also get into one's genes?—but damn, I could not pursue it now. What was that about Dr. Deere and a thorough check-up? Was Randy closing in? And then a further interruption: the phone rang again.

Calm down, I said to myself. I picked it up, hoping for a sweet reconciliation with Gwendolyn. I said, "Hello," with no trepidation.

"Hello, Gerry." It was Manuel. "How're you feeling?"

"It's time I told you," I began.

"What?" he said in his specially serious manner. "Tell me, I want to hear. That's why I'm calling."

"I don't like a son of mine calling me Gerry," I said, not realizing that he had thought I was going to talk about my health. "I never liked it; it cost me a lot to bring you boys up—I want all the honorifics."

"Absolutely," he said. His voice relaxed. "I agree."

"And certainly not with a name that's not mine. You wanna call me by my given name—it's Germán."

"Yes, yes," he said with an enthusiasm that surprised me. Especially since nothing ever elated him. "Insist on the Spanish. Did you see *el General Lister* died?"

Another surprise. "You know about him?" I noted he pronounced the name as if it were English.

"The only openly Communist general of the Spanish Republic," he said.

"Enrique Lister," I said. "He died?"

"Let's talk about that," he said in his equable, even tone. He paused, however, and added, "Father."

I was puzzled. "What about? That he died?"

"The Spanish Communists, the Republic," he said. "The Civil War. I'll come down for lunch. How does that sound to you?"

I said, "Are you writing a book?"

"Actually, I wrote most of a short story, based on something you said about your father..."

"*Your* grandfather," I said.

"Absolutely, my grandfather," he said more quickly than usual. "That he was Galician and how that was special..."

"Lister was Galician," I said, as if I were arguing.

"It said so in the obituary," Manuel said.

"That's good," I said. "If ever I get an obituary, I want it to say I was the son of a *gallego*."

"I will make sure it does," he said. "Maybe you're free for dinner tonight—what do you say? Sylvie will cover for me. And we can talk."

"There's no need to break any dates," I said.

"Oh, it's a family party—her family—and I am happy to break it," he said. "I want to hear everything you know about Spain and those Spaniards in your hometown..."

"No hurry," I said, but I did not mean to put him off; I was eager to see him. In fact, my three sons are the most interesting people I know. "Another day, when it's easier on you. It doesn't have to be tonight. We can talk on the phone."

"I do want to see you to look at you, I must confess," he said. "I talked to Dr. Deere."

"What is this?" I exclaimed.

"Randy was worried about your physical well-being..."

"He talked to Deere, too, he told me," I said. "The whole thing's absurd...you can ask me if you wanna know."

"He didn't talk to Deere," Manuel said. "He hoped I would."

"Then he did not talk to Deere?" I said.

Manuel made a negative sound. "He has a difficult time when a situation is too emotionally laden."

I said, "For crissakes."

"Randy thinks you're holding back on what's ailing you."

It made me mad to hear. "He does, does he?"

"Randy believes you turned into a stoic Wasp during those years in Vermont." There was a certain amusement in his voice. "And Dr. Deere did tell me that you're a very private person and that he had to respect that."

"Private person!"

"I'm sorry to have repeated that. I know how you are about trendy expressions."

"He's a fine doctor; I'm lucky to have him."

"Absolutely," he said, marking time until he thought of the best way to ask the inevitable question. He hates trendy expressions, too. "So, what's wrong?"

"Spaniards are as dignified as any Wasp. More so. Randy was guilty of harboring an enthymeme when he said that."

"What's that?" Manuel asked, and I could hear the enthusiasm that overtakes him with matters of language. "An enthymeme?"

"A suppressed premise," I explained with a certain hauteur. "The premise in this statement about Wasps is Randy's hidden acceptance of a racist view of Spaniards."

"Great! I'm going to use that, a fine stiletto of a word," he said. "I'll pick you up in a taxi at your place a half-hour from now and we'll go on to a new restaurant in Tribeca not too many people know about, and I'm sure there's an enthymeme in that."

Especially when I saw the restaurant's name—Class Act. But it was quiet inside and hardly any customer could be called a yuppie. They knew him, and a young man in black and a neat ponytail led us without discussion to a table far from the entrance, the kitchen and the bar. Manuel took for granted neither of us would want a hard drink, but he consulted with me about the wine. He was familiar with their list. What did I know? And why care tonight? The number 3 had kicked in, and it was easy to nod to anything he proposed. I did not worry that it might make me groggy; again, I wasn't going to drive home. He settled on a chardonnay from a small California vineyard.

"Just don't make it Chilean," I said. "Or have we given up on that boycott?"

"Ah," he said happily—this was such a natural lead-in to the Spain of the Thirties.

"Nor chilled," I added.

"We want the full bouquet tonight," he said, and he immediately sped into the subject of Spain with a question about Galician local wines. He had done his homework; he had read an old article of mine on Santiago de Compostela. He asked me if it was true that they are fresher than beaujolais nouveau and do not travel.

"That's what my cousin in Niveiro said and he kept a tavern," I told him, although this, too, was in the article. "Even if transported only to Madrid they lose their body, their bouquet, their mystique. He didn't use all those words, he simply said spoiled."

"Madrid!" Manuel said, getting on to what really interested him. "Did that hotel really exist? The one in *The Fifth Column*? Should I trust Hemingway?"

"He had an attitude," I said.

He raised his eyebrows to show he knew.

"Not too bad a one," I said, "even if all of it taken together puts him beyond the pale with the kids. He understood the kids of his time, the ones who went to fight in Spain."

And so we were launched, via Papa's tribute to the Abraham Lincoln Brigade, onto the grandest subject of this century—that Civil War and its lead players. And the rank and file you see in Cartier Bresson's and Capa's photographs, the peasants in Malraux's documentary. A people unequaled in defeat, they seemed never to have counted the cost. Manuel had heard of the people I named—Orwell, of course, César Vallejo, Neruda, Machado, Alberti—but did not know the poems our own Philip Levine has written about his beloved anarchists.

"So many poets!" Manuel said.

"Yes, we mustn't forget that it began with the death of Lorca and ended with that of Angel Hernández."

He scribbled in a small leather notebook from Smythson's which he kept open on the table while we ate and drank. "Angel Hernández?" he said. "I don't know about him."

"A young poet from Murcia. He began writing as a teenage shepherd boy, religious poems they were. He became an open Communist and was taken by the fascists..." I had to stop a moment. I had not thought about him in a long time.

Manuel said in his careful voice, "No one says fascist anymore."

"I'll tell you something I have never used. Hernández died in a Franco prison, of tuberculosis brought on by the beatings they gave him. With the blood from one of his hemorrhages he wrote on the wall—Say goodbye to the wheat and the sun for me."

"Ah," Manuel said.

It gave me time to look away and hide my unexpected tears, so unexpected they burned my eyelids. How intensely Angel Hernández had lived his life; his example made it possible for me to admit I wanted more than anything to continue to live. I must not give way to my Death Sentence, make a pact with the devil, rather; anything, but stick around to have my say. Write my farewell on the wall. Imprecations, more likely. Yes. I turned to Manuel—I think I was smiling—and said, "And what is it you gonna write?"

"Something short, direct, open-hearted. Like *Un Coeur Simple*," he said. "But I need to know everything about Spain for it to have any authority."

Yes.

Manuel added, "Flaubert must have known about the bad things to be able to write about a pure soul, about goodness itself."

We did not drink as much as we intended. The talk lifted our spirits as much as the wine. We were very happy, and very close, not like father and son but like equals. Another incident I had not used and now told Manuel about: when I went ashore in Toulon during the Southern France invasion, all the Maquis I met were Spanish Republicans. They wanted to cross the border and bring down Franco, but Winston Churchill and FDR did not let them. I still believe that if the Spanish Republicans had won, my life would have been profoundly different. I still believe that conversations like this, preoccupations like ours, made for true happiness. Ah, politics! Ah, art!

The truth is, I am not much like a father with any of my sons. Tony takes no avuncular advice and laughs good-naturedly at my sallies, so that I am sometimes happy he lives way off in the Hamptons. Randy is closest and lies the most, a friend and as untrustworthy as most friends are. But I am as one with Manuel, in literature. We were both eager to get home; he to make notes or maybe write one more page to impel him in the morning, me to find a devil who would help me. Was it Manuel who inspired it? Was it Spain? I longed to live longer. Give me more years, Satan, give me ten.

Manuel made the cab wait while he walked me up to the canopy of my building. "Oh," he said, suddenly recalling his mission, "you feeling okay?"

"Extremely well," I said, and I did, at that moment and all the way upstairs.

The answering machine was blinking. I felt too finely tuned and sure of what I would do to turn it on and let the world in. With neither painkiller nor sleeping pill I floated into sleep. I awoke in thirty minutes—a small clock by my bed glows green in the dark—and asked myself, What if it's the dear girl? From the plane? Why not? I jumped out of bed and hit the button on the machine and of course it was Billie Gladiola. *You got one of those? I've given in, too. What about the Clint Eastwood? Call me.* No! I cried aloud.

I turned back in the dark and bumped into a lamp, then a chair, and fell forward into the bed. Oh, the devil take me, I said aloud again. I breathed heavily with frustration, until I head her voice whisper, *It's you I love.* And no more. There had been no introductory greeting. Just *It's you I love.* Was she in the room? But then the beep of the machine signing off sounded. *It's you I love.* Not Stacey, not Thom, not Randy. I crawled up and laid on the pillow and stretched out and told myself, do not think about it, lie back, enjoy the sensation. I went into flotation once more. I said softly, It's you I love, and, with my arms flung out on either side of me, let myself go off into blessed sleep.

◇

I am rather good at getting people who do not know me to do things they are not supposed to do. Minor things, of course. Occasionally to break routine regulations, like persuading subway token vendors to grant me senior citizen fares without showing them my medicare card. I became a steadfast viewer of a TV private-eye series because its hero was adept at this sort of ruse. He carried a small handprinter in his car and manufactured calling cards for whatever the unpredictable occasion demanded. I began the campaign whose outlines I had worked out—as I do all my stories—with a similar minor deception—as all fiction does—less culpable, however, than those of my favorite detective. If I was going to live, I would have to find someone to exorcise my cancer, and where does one find this necromancer but in a hospital. Ah, but... and this is when lying comes in handy.

After coffee the next morning I sat at my desk, got a pad and pen ready and called one I had carefully picked. A huge one like New York Hospital—notice I said "like

New York Hospital." I am giving you no names; I don't want lawsuits for me or my heirs. Another hospital which would qualify is Presbyterian Medical Center, but that's too far uptown. The taxi fare alone would kill me if the DS did not, for I could no longer climb the subway stairs or walk farther than the couple of blocks to Washington Square. In medical conglomerates like these there are likely to be medical projects of all kinds in progress; or not progressing, for that matter, in a sought-for stasis. I imagined catacombs, cobwebbed corridors, project directors whose work has for long not been closely supervised. Whatever its real name, I called it the Rumanian Waterworks.

Another virtue of the Rumanian Waterworks is that Doctors Deere and Hamilton do not practice there. For all I knew, too, Hamilton's colleagues at his hospital might all look at my PSAs and scans and agree with him that nothing could be done about my aggressive and metastasized prostate. Hope for the best and when the pain becomes unbearable, remove my testicles. That was his game plan. I was looking for another approach, as they also say in the advertising agencies (real necromancers, these Joes), but how to come by it I should have to play by ear. I said briskly to the operator, "Urology Department, please."

She replied as briskly, "Clinical or laboratory?"

"Laboratory, thank you," I said. And advised myself, Keep it light, don't sound earnest. Some other person in me said, But it's a matter of life and death. And the me with the phone in hand said, That's right, more reason to keep it light.

A male answered at the urological laboratory, but only with a "Yes?"

They are harder to fool—males tend to be hard-hearted—but I did not hesitate; I was a male myself. "Actually, I hope your laboratory includes oncologists. That's the kind of urologist I'm trying to reach," I said, making myself sound like an unthreatening cretin.

"Yes," he said, but it sounded more like a question than assent.

"Let me explain," I continued, this time also sounding a note of apology. I told him I was looking for a particular urological oncologist. I was given his name but had misplaced it. "But I have only to hear it to remember."

"I beg your pardon?" he said, and there was no hope of assent this time.

My job was clear: I must soften him up before I dared ask him to read me the list of his research oncologists. "I am doing a piece for the *New York Times*," I confided, "and I need to talk to this doctor—not, of course, for attribution but background.

It gave him pause, as I had hoped and expected.

"Of course, if he allows me to quote him," I added; and by this time I had taken on a slight English accent. "I should be very pleased."

He said, "How can I help?"

He was hooked. The *Times* always get to them; it had gained me entrée in South America into government palaces to interview jittery colonels and stuffy ministers who wanted a good press from the only newspaper in the United States that matters in the rest of the world.

I suggested, "If you would read me the names of the urological oncologists on your roster?..."

Another pause, but there was no resistance, no heaviness in it. "Let me see," he said.

"Or is it too long a list? Would you prefer to mail..."

"No, it is not too long. I am thinking," he said. That is what he said: that he was thinking, I would not have let anyone else get away with that sort of talk. "Let me read it to you now, it is not feasible to mail it."

"I see," I said with all the sympathetic understanding I could fake.

He read in a precise uninflected manner. Every ethnic group seemed included in the first eight or so names. None that struck me as simpático. Then he read, "Mefisto..."

"Stop, that's he." I took a wild stab: "And his given name is Adolf?"

"Yes," he replied, and there was an eerie tremor on the wire, I swear; it emanated from him and it could build into laughter or sharpen into a shriek.

"Is he in?" I said. Notice that I did not ask, Will he see me? That is another gambit I picked up when playing the journalist. Not see a byline writer from the *Times*?—*mon Dieu*!

The voiced modulated into open amusement. "I am Dr. Mefisto."

What do I do now? Brazen it out: "You run an old-fashioned one-man operation?" I chuckled to show I was kidding; I could always take it back.

"We shall talk about that," he said, still amused. "You are calling from downtown?"

Did I hear a Middle European accent? Or was it merely his somewhat stiff locution? "Yes," I said. "When..."

"Permit me," he said peremptorily. "Take a taxi. You shall be here in twenty minutes. I can give you an hour, or close to an hour. That will be sufficient."

"You're the boss," I said. "Thanks."

"You take the elevator to the ninth floor. You will find me in Nine West Low."

"Low?" I said.

"You take steps down. You will find me."

"I have a lot of questions," I said, to warm him up for the real reason I called. "Some personal."

"I beg your pardon?" he said in his old tone, all the fun gone from his voice.

"Personal with me, that is," I said.

"Your time is up, Mr. Morán," he said and hung up.

I'm on a roll, I told myself in the taxi, I'm on a roll. I am pushing all the right buttons. Loathsome expressions. I was almost there when it occurred to me that I had not given him my name. Of course, I had. I let the phone conversation play itself back. No, I had not. Forget it, I decided, I'm on a roll.

I knew where I was going. I did not stop at the desk where outpatients stood obediently giving their names and appointment hours to the female clerks who had already lost, though it was still morning, whatever freshness their greetings contained when they began the day. A male nurse just past their station asked if he could help me. I pointed ahead. "The men's room," I said, and he nodded with a slight smile, and I continued to the end of the corridor. I had taken a chance, but there it was. I needed to urinate, a constant condition with me, but beyond the men's room three steps led down to a solid door.

I turned the knob and pushed against it, and it sighed when it let me in. I walked into a white Formica short corridor brilliantly lit, indirectly so that I did not feel assaulted but illuminated in a curiously uplifting way. A dark figure opened a door whose seams were invisible in the solid white wall. It must be Dr. Mefisto: he looked like Bela Lugosi with his eyebrows flying out satanically. Maybe not Hungarian or Rumanian but perhaps Bosnian or Croatian or Lebanese or Kurd. He was a national on the edge of Western civilization, abutting on but not of our world. I was happy about that; his person played to all my expectations and harmless prejudices, but a mystery remained: I could not entirely place him.

"Germán Morán," he said, and held the door open for me. I kept my face towards him as I went into his office in ambulant fascination. The pupils of his eyes were opaque, totally black. The office chairs (two) and the desk (a writing surface) and the filing cabinets were white, too, each the sort of thing Breuer and Gropius brought to America from the Bauhaus.

"Needless to say, I am very grateful," I began.

As on the phone, he interrupted, this time without words. He pointed me to a chair on the nearer side of the writing table. I should not, otherwise, have known which one to take. There was nothing on the writing surface. There was also nothing to distinguish the chair, in looks or position, as the one for visitors. He said blandly, "You have come to see me about yourself and not for any journalism."

His questions were always statements.

"I am a writer," I said, and squared my shoulders. "Everything is grist for my mill."

I stared at him to show I was not letting him have the ascendancy. He merely looked at me. Rather, he kept his eyes on me, but since no light was reflected in them, God knows what he was looking at.

"For journalism or for fiction," I added, with a little less spirit.

He looked at his watch—he was always to show that he was not above the banal gesture or expression—and waited, resting one hand on the other atop the desk.

"Okay," I said, and confessed.

He asked me to begin at the beginning and to tell him everything. All the details. I'm rather good at that, and I should have settled back and expatiated leisurely, except that Breuer designs do not allow you. Two or three times he told me to repeat a comment either Deere or Hamilton had made. Mostly about scans and blood tests. Only once did he show any emotion. That was of amusement, of course; I cannot imagine compassion or warmth from him. It came when I told him that Hamilton had said all that could be done for me was castration.

"He said that," he said, but I knew it was a question.

"Actually, he said, when the time comes I can remove your testicles—it's a very simple procedure—and you will feel no more pain after that. That's how he phrased it."

I looked closely at him to see if he agreed about the enormity of such a cure.

He said, "And you said."

I shook my head. "I said I didn't like the idea."

That was when his pale face broke into a smile. "You would miss them," he said, and lifted his hands from the table for emphasis. "They have been in the family too long."

He surprised me. If he could smile, I could plead. "Help me," I said. "I was ready to go when he first told me five months ago, but now..." I leaned forward a little. "Can you help me?"

He nodded. "We do not cut off anything," he said. "We give you hormonal treatment."

"And?" I said.

"You will be well," he said. He got up and went over to a cabinet so white it had been invisible until then. He opened a slim drawer. "We start today," he said. He shook some brown and yellow capsules into a vial. "You take these today and tomorrow, and the next morning you come to see me"—he looked at his watch—"at this time and I shall give you an injection."

"Of hormones?" I said.

"I can explain, but you are not equipped to understand," he said. "You get an injection every four weeks."

"And?" I said again.

"Who can predict how long you will live," he said. "Ten years, it could be. And with a good quality of life."

I was in danger of crying. I said, "How can I repay you?"

He did not reply then. He took several blood samples. He watched my blood flow into the vials he slid on to the inserted needle. Twice he removed the vial and replaced it with another. I watched him, just in case. He said nothing then or later about Hamilton and Deere. I understood it was up to me to tell them or not. He said, "There is no one here today to take your non-vital statistics. No forms to complete. You will come see me at the same time every four weeks for an injection. Remember that. There is no one to give you a little appointment card either."

He dismissed me by opening the seamless door to the brilliant corridor.

"Doctor," I began, but did not have to ask again.

"Someday, years from now," he said, and lifted his black eyebrows slightly, "you give your body to my students."

I nodded. It was no use being witty with him; he had no talent for give-and-take. "Yes," I said solemnly.

He closed the door behind me. I took a few steps to the big one leading into the hospital. I said aloud but not too loud, "I have made a pact with Modern Science." I should have said that to Mefisto; he would have appreciated it. But before I got to the elevator I decided not. He was a humorless devil of a fellow, and I'd have to watch my ways with him. He was in the business of saving life (I don't believe he thought much about individual lives) and could not care less for the insights of writers like me who are in the business of tearing it apart. Yet, if he was a powerful devil—and I already banked on that—would he not exact a sacrifice? But Modern Science has no hell, so what can it condemn me to in exchange for ten years of life? How would I pay? I had no right to live the fable and accept only its happy plot elements.

I pondered these matters in the taxi that appeared downstairs as if by magic. I also took out my trusty little notebook and pen and wrote down the dates I would be returning to see Mefisto. My memory no longer hung onto practical facts the way it did in my journalism days. I am more at ease with generalizations and theories, and that is how I spent the while as the driver zigzagged west and south down to the Village. The side streets in the Twenties, some of which I had never walked, were dotted with specialty shops—coffee beans from all over the world, chocolate, French country furniture, antiquarian bookstores, a pink window dedicated to embroidery—places that could only exist in New York City. Like Nine West Low. Magic corners in the frantic terrain of the metropolis. I would not tell Deere and Hamilton about Mefisto. I'm on a roll, I told myself; I'm not taking them on it.

A corner of my mind remained untamed and skeptical. Would I only be required to pay with my old carcass? There must be a proviso in small print in my pact with Modern Science whose import I had yet to hit upon. Would it leap out at me like a dagger in a funhouse? As certain as Randy's return from L.A. The expectation would keep me alert, provide the page-turning suspense of my coming days. Oh, nonsense, I said to myself, it was just a doctor's visit. I felt the vial of capsules in my shirt pocket and tittered. No, it had really happened. I had pushed the right buttons today. I leaned back and listened to my DS recede like a silent but palpable tide. I am on a roll, happier with the phrase this time. Happy, indeed.

Peace

Just as there are priorities in life, choices we must make about what comes first, so are there in narration. I cannot say to you, You are not equipped—*I* must equip you. That's what a storyteller does, equip the reader to follow all the turns and arrive at all the right conclusions. But I'm not going to doggedly describe and I don't want you to slavishly follow. Should we go back to the Rumanian Water Works Low two days later and recount how I coyly lowered my pants far enough for Mefisto to inject me in the left buttock, or should I rather return to my darling Gwendolyn and her further adventures in the world of drama and how they impinged on me? What about Randy and Thom and Stacey? I cannot keep them waiting in the wings meanwhile. And Manuel? Wasn't he too interesting to drop at this point or for good? Fatso, I'm sure, you can do without.

The problem for me—and I admit it is mine not yours—is how to keep these stars in my firmament flashing in the middle and far distance and along the horizon and yet allow you to follow their trajectory as closely as you should like. I am not interested in dazzling everybody, like a vulgar juggler at the circus. Or in noting every detail like a sociologist. I am a teller of tales. Let's be honest—of *my* tale. And if your attention strays, well, it strays. If I lose you…there are worse things in this life.

Like the unexpected, the one person I had not thought I would have to keep you up on. Billie Gladiola. She was on the answering machine. *What the hell is this! The goddam movie goes on at three o'clock and that's my last chance to catch it this week. Get off your skinny ass and call me.* I called her. If I was gonna live I had to spare some time for her.

The moment she heard my voice, she gloated. Rather, took on a fat, tolerant tone. "I'm shaking you out of your doldrums," she said. "It's a danger of old age, petrifying."

"Let's keep this impersonal," I said, eschewing my gentlemanly manner with the female sex. "No comments about my butt."

Ha-ha, she said.

"In a half-hour I'll pick you up in a taxi, so you won't be seen heading there," I said, when she told me the movie was playing at that complex on Third Avenue, too far for me to walk. "This is not a date, so be there on the sidewalk on time."

"I've organized too many demonstrations to be accused of that..."

"For crissakes, don't look like you're going to a demonstration either," I said, and went ha-ha myself this time.

The phone rang before I could walk away from it. It was Tony. "My God, I don't believe it," I said. "I heard from Manuel yesterday."

"He told me you had a great time," he said. "I'm coming to town tomorrow for an afternoon appointment. How about lunch? I need the sort of parenting you don't get in the Hamptons. I don't want to sound like a swinger, but I hear the St. Regis has a fine new pastry chef."

"Just pay," I said, "and you won't qualify as a swinger."

His voice became soft in the attempt to sound neutral. "Didn't Manny pay?"

I made a noise: I wasn't giving him any ammunition. I said no more, and I had the feeling he was smiling at the other end. We were at a standstill for a moment. Finally, I said, "Yes, but he didn't leave a good tip."

"We don't want to encourage the masses," he said.

I listened for some concern about my health while he went into details about time and place, but I heard none. Maybe I was wrong about Randy beating the bushes.

When I closed the apartment door behind me, I head my phone ring. I did not go back for it, but I put my ear to the door and discovered I could not hear the answering machine come on. I told myself that I should adjust the volume when I got back. I had made sure some time ago that I could hear it in the john if I kept the door open. We used to listen at keyholes: this is what the electronic age has done for me.

I had taken a codeine to be okay for the next three hours. I'll skip ahead and tell you that three days after I got Mefisto's first injection my aches and pains began to disappear. Only the regular bad-back pangs and occasional sinus headaches remained. That was five days away, of course, but it was not until a couple of days beyond that when I walked up to Barnes & Noble that I noticed. For the moment, codeine was my only love.

I said nothing sharp to Billie about having to buy her popcorn and Coke, both medium-size but still huge anyway. I am a gentleman, after all. But when she gripped my knee as the first minor character was blown away in close-up, I said, "You groping me?" and tapped the top of her hand unlovingly.

"Just for that, you're gonna have to take me to a McDonald's I know," she said. "It's hidden away on 14th Street."

"Shush," someone behind us said.

She turned her head and said, "You kidding?"

They moved away. She shushed them as they bumped into seats on the way to the aisle, and I forgave her everything. Or maybe the codeine had really kicked in. She offered me the popcorn by holding it in my direction and elbowing me. I shook my head, and she said, "Good," and I didn't hear from her until the movie was over. She did not spill any of it and she ate it all and crunched the ice from the Coke in her mouth.

Her first words were, "I loved it, didn't you?"

I shook my head to that, too.

"How can you not like Clint Eastwood!"

I said, "His ass is too skinny."

She elbowed me again. "Now you know my secret passion."

Being with her was like acting in a sitcom: not a moment was allowed to relax into healthy boredom or real inconsequentiality. A laugh a minute and a *pronunciamento* every five. Whereas Tony (who did pick me up the next day) was first rate at light-hearted inattention, at marking time playfully. There was also a beguiling signal in his manner that he would argue about nothing you said, that he would go along with you if you felt the least bit strongly. He would go along for now, anyway. "Really?" (said mildly) was his most stringent demurrer, and then it sounded more like interested surprise than disbelief. He was the carrier, I liked to say, of uninherited characteristics. If only he would pass it on to all mankind.

I once said this in the presence of one of Fatso's friends, and she said in that ghastly manner that feminists of a certain ilk have, "Are women included in this mankind?" I replied, "No, that would be an impossible achievement for any."

Billie put up no resistance to my dropping her off at home immediately after the movie. (Awful, by the way, not to be discussed.) "On second thought, let me off at Sixth," she said. "There's a Village Forestation meeting at PS 11 I promised to put in an appearance at...you're invited if you wanna."

I shook my head once more. "I'm too politically correct as it is," I explained.

I got out and opened the door for her. She hadn't been as bad as I had expected. She said, "Hey, you got away with no McDonald's." I gave her a nod and a wink. She looked up and down Sixth Avenue conspiratorially. "Tell nobody about today."

I could have fed her a sitcom line, but instead just went ha-ha. You gotta give her credit, she walked away without any attempt to lay any grappling hooks on me for another date. And I went on home feeling not too bad.

There were messages from Gwendolyn and Randy to which I had a thousand reactions, but I prefer to get Tony out of the way first. Not exactly out of the way. I see him a couple of times a year, but I enjoy him and wish it were more often. I don't needle him about it, however, as Fatso used to.

Well, this time I did. He was sporting a beard, so I said, "Who gave you that beard? Your brothers never told me—I see why."

He was in a chauffeured car, and the driver got out and opened the door for me. I think he bowed slightly.

Tony had stayed inside and held out a hand to help me in." I thought it might be fun," he said.

"I didn't ask why," I said. "I know you're not hiding weak mandibles, but why all over your face and not your neck? You going Hamptons on me?"

The driver was behind the wheel and kept a straight face. I was playing up to him, but I guess he didn't know it. He drove on and never looked back until we got to the hotel. It was not the St. Regis. A little farther uptown—the Sherry Netherlands? I won't say. Again, I don't want any lawsuits, even if all I say about it is that the pastry was indeed good.

Tony knew I was playing up to him as well, my youngest son whom I had always most indulged. He was willing to go along, obliging fellow that he is. "I had a beard there, too," he said, and gave it a quick rub, "but it got too hot. It forced me to hold my head up and back to get the air—ventilate it, I mean—and that gave me a haughty look."

I liked that. I placed a hand on his shoulder.

Tony cocked his head in the fashion he had described, and said, "You have to appear democratic in the Hamptons."

"Also rich," I said, and he nodded mock-solemnly.

We bantered all the way up to the hotel's side-street entrance. He said, "Two thirty," to the driver and no more, as if to the manner born. As soon as we were out of his hearing, he looked at me with affection, placed a hand on my withered biceps and said, "You look fine, Dad."

I said, "I hate health talk, I'm gonna order everything on the menu—I hope you're on an expense account."

I did not ask him about his family. His wife, Myra, was Main Line Philadelphia, and she took a risk marrying him. The only other good thing I can say about her is that she was superb at checkmating Fatso. They had two girls who might someday be interesting but certainly were not now. They were a couple of years from puberty and light years before their intelligence would show. I asked him about his work.

"A little rustic cabin in the mountains for a fellow who's sick of the Atlantic—that's just off the drawing board and being costed by the construction people," he began, was not encouraged by the look on my face, and decided to bring his reply to a quick close. "And today I'm looking at one of those twenty-room apartments on Fifth Avenue—to see if it can be made liveable."

"Your great-grandfather would've redesigned it with a bomb," I said.

He looked pleased, not that politics meant a thing to him. "I tell people that I'm descended from strong characters," he said, "and that way they never complain about the preliminary costs. Later..."

I broke in. "No writing?" I said.

"That's nice. I know you believe writing is my real work," he said. He feared I'd fight about that, so he tapped my arm to get me to hold it. A waiter bent over slightly in his direction. "What if we order a bottle of wine instead of...hard drinks?"

I nodded to his question and to his comment.

"You know, architecture is a lot of fun," he said, waved the sommelier over, and asked him for something or the other. I didn't hear; I was thinking what a bore I had become. Finally, when he saw he had my attention, he said, "Too," and winked.

"Fun?" I said. "Architecture was man's first..." and stopped myself. "Oh, the hell with that. None of you need lectures."

He was a good fellow; he said, "I don't think about large matters, like Manny." I couldn't tell if he was boasting; he certainly was not apologizing. "And I don't move fast, like Randy." He half-closed his eyes. "I wish I were like them."

I looked around at the innards of our alcove, and I could tell that he readied himself, ever so slightly, for my one-liner. I almost didn't say, "This is the way Jonah must have felt."

He nodded rather than smiled. "I'm afraid I'm a bit superficial, Dad," he said. I saw him think about taking that back. Instead, he blinked and nodded once more. "I'm all right, though, aren't I, Dad?"

He had not been that earnest with me since he was thirteen and had asked me about sex. I could have cried. "The visit to Mefisto had unhinged me—or was it Gwendolyn? Tony let his eyes water and did not look away from me. I wish I knew how I returned his gaze—if there was any reassuring expression on my face, that is—for I was thinking he was still unformed after all.

I did say, "You are more than all right."

Going home alone in the limo down Fifth Avenue, I thought of many beautiful things I could have said. He had insisted on the limo taking me home first while he walked up Fifth to the apartment, and as he waved me away after asking me once more if I was okay, he seemed as light-hearted as ever. I looked at him from the corner while the chauffeur waited for the light to turn left, and I saw him pause under the canopy of the Hotel Pierre and look towards its doors. Why should he be a writer? Why should I prod him?

The limo crept down Fifth and I had plenty of time to figure out that I hadn't been so smart: his life must be in turmoil and I had not thought to ask. Did he go into the Hotel Pierre? He had told the driver to pick him up later at the apartment. My thoughts should not have been this suspicious and insensitive and egotistical after having talked to Gwendolyn on the phone the previous day. That is why I skipped ahead to Tony and now go back to the darling Irish lass who churned me up and opened me up and caused me to recall my life in Tampa as part of what is now called an extended family, in and out of my aunts' homes—everyone's on the block, in fact—where there was no room for escape from others. Not that you could not be fiercely self-concerned, but we pummeled each other with our wants and were the better for it. And if I learned that Tony did go into the Hotel Pierre, it was she, the darling lass, who gave me the breadth to wish him fun not tears.

◈

Gwendolyn immediately asked, "Are you all right? I left you with all those crazy fellows..." She knew how to pause and yet keep the ball in her court—that's a mixed metaphor, I think. Anyway, I could not speak without feeling that I was interrupting her. I waited. "Sweetheart?" she called out.

"Yes," I said, and it seemed to me that I had failed her—that is, had not responded right. More than silence had been called for. What a wonderful gift she has! The gift of communication without words. The lack of it in us writers makes us bumbling and inexact, no matter how we fiddle with every sentence. "Yes," I repeated.

She laughed a laugh that did not get away from her.

"Oh, I don't mean that I agree they're crazy," I said, then found the wit to add, "Except Owen."

"You're going to look out for him, aren't you, sweetheart?" Her pause this time told me I was supposed to reply in the same heartfelt foolish manner.

Where was she drawing me? I hate kids. Wasn't she merely the girl down the hall who had stopped to talk to me a couple of times? When did I become a nursemaid? I let bad second thoughts like those pass me by. I love her, that's the important fact about her. "Of course, of course," I said happily.

"He has just grown out of the terrible twos," she said, as if pleading. "Now his real character is ready to be shaped. He won't be saying no, no, to everything."

She wanted more of an answer. "Yes, I will help," I said, in something of a rush. "I told Stacey that..."

"Oh, that is such a relief to know, such a blessing," she said, a little breathless herself. "It frees me from... Oh, I wish it were a year ago!"

"A year ago?" I said, off balance again.

"So you could be his godfather," she explained.

I did not know what to make of that. Me, a godfather?

She explained further, "He was baptized a year ago." She paused and thought she was clearing any remaining confusion by adding, "I know it's a little late for a Catholic, but I waited until I found the one right place—I wasn't going to have him baptized in the true church."

"No?" I said, but did not really require any explanation.

"I've said something wrong," she said. "I take it back. It's silly of me to be anti anything."

"You mean anti-Catholic?" I said. "I don't mind that at all. In fact..."

"This was an Episcopalian minister and an actor! Wonderful at playing Shaw, where you need actors who can articulate. He can boom, too! And the ceremony was as elaborate as in our church. Even Moira liked it and she is a Catholic nun." She made a funny noise: laughter caught in the throat, an old actor's trick. "I must be very nervous, I'm talking such foolishness. But I do mean I wish you were Owen's godfather. I made a mistake there. I thought I knew him well; he was our landlord, but..."

I waited, but for the moment nothing came through.

I asked, just to ask, "Who is Moira?"

"I didn't tell you about Aunt Moira?" she said. "My mother's oldest sister, one of ten... She became a nun so she could get out of the house. She had to get special dispensation to come to Owen's baptism. So she got out of one house into another. Oh, dear..."

This time there were vibes—she had not finished—and I stayed quiet.

"Sweetheart?" she said in a sharp voice. "Is Randy amorous?"

"Amorous?"

"I'm so old-fashioned..."

This is it, this is it, my heart said and began fluttering. The terrible chords from *Carmen* were about to strike; the Mefisto magic dispersed. I controlled my quaver and asked, "Apt to fall in love, you mean?"

Her voice became small, too. "I guess I mean sexy."

Stay away from him, I wanted to say; I wanted to say that and many other things along the same line. But Randy is my son, and my life had not prepared me for a situation like this. I had no ready-made phrases, not even a knowing chuckle. He had won her, I feared.

"Don't say anything," she said. "It's the auditions, they're making me crazy. It's just that Randy called yesterday and asked me out to dinner. I had just come from a totally unprepared audition: they handed me this script and said, here, read. I didn't even know the character's name. I told them that...and then they informed me it was a voice-over. A commercial—and I'm searching for a character! Can you imagine! And afterwards my agent gave me a real script for an audition today, so I wanted to stay home and go over it...I said no to him. Randy, I mean. You understand, don't you?"

I said, "I'm sure he also understands about auditions," my voice strong again, my heart still unsure of itself.

"Yes, yes, of course, and you'll explain to him so he won't be angry," she pled. "You get so untrusting in this profession. I thought that he...forget it, tell me about yourself."

I wished I could. All about my pact, how I was going to live forever, that she could really count on me now. But how could I? Hadn't my love for her been all in my mind, undeclared and mute? I couldn't—shouldn't—have the nerve to announce it like this on the phone. Anyway, what I was mostly feeling—reveling in, actually—was that she had turned Randy down. All my suspicions were wrong, pre-Mefisto, I told myself, having now entered a new world of happiness. Acceptance, like Mahler's in *Das Lied von der Erde*. Accept what comes your way. I could have sung that plaintive ending to her. *Ewig*, *ewig*: forever, forever.

I told her I was well, that Thom had come by with Owen. They were walking up and down the hall and I happened to open my door. "We are taking a little walk, Thom said, and Owen here wants to visit Dad," I reported.

"Oh, that's good, Thom is wonderful with him," she said. "All gays are great with kids."

"Yes," I said, and every construction you could put to that one-word reply was a lie: 1) that I knew who or what is great for kids, 2) that it would be good if I were in contact with Owen or any kid, 3) that all or any gay is great with them, and 4) (and rankest lie) that I knew Thom is gay.

"He's a character," I said, to sound even more knowing.

A kind of buzz started in my head. Thom is gay. Jesus. Not to have known made me feel naive, a response I had not experienced in decades and would not have confessed to anyone.

"That's it!" she exclaimed. "That's the secret to doing voice-overs. It's a character saying it, it's not a mellifluous voice. You see what talking to you does for me?"

I said something or the other, but I was looking at my apartment door and remembering Thom the first time he entered, erect and neat, a compact bundle of muscles. He was a nice, attractive fellow. Let him do what he wants when he makes love. A couple of images of what that was stumbled against each other in my mind, but I felt less of a greenhorn for the thought. Still, I confess, a bit jarred.

She was saying, "I can't wait to get back. I have so much to learn from you. Will you teach me? Will you put up with me, sweetheart?"

"Well, my dear," I said, "it's good for me to talk to you..." I stopped, to keep myself from saying I love her.

"You mean it!" she said. "Tell me you mean it!"

I said, "You make me feel young again." Next time I'd tell her I love her. Not just yet.

"O-o-o-oo," she held on to the syllable as if it were the opening note of a love song in an ancient operetta.

But we had gone through all this before. So, I said, "I love you," and goddamit I held my breath like a sixteen-year old. "There," I added.

◇

When I hung up, she was still in a kind of swoon. How could I believe my declaration of love has this effect on a young girl? We were only on the phone, after all. My speech couldn't be followed by the kind of grappling that her response invited. She must know it was an impossibility. What could I give her—on the phone or off? But none of these doubts gave off the slightest sadness: I was in a state myself. I moved from study to living room to kitchen like a floating ingenue in happy levitation.

I needed an extra digitalis to slow down my pulse and also strengthen it. I went to the apartment door and just before I opened it realized that I was looking for company and that this was something I could not confess to anyone. Not to Stacey, not to Thom, whom it would embarrass me to tell. I laughed at the thought of relating it to Ernestine Puglia. Or Billie Gladiola. Certainly not the boys. Who was left—my literary agent?

I could tell the Italian Old Gent in the park, that's who I could tell. I turned back into the apartment, and put on the tweed cap I bought in Dublin. Ah, if only I were there and could go into a pub; there is nothing you cannot tell an Irishman in a pub! Thus armed with hope and gladness, I took a taxi to Washington Square. Too many aches, my joints too creaky to walk that far. It was still thirty-six hours before I got my first injection, and then it would be a few days for my aches to go away. Dr. Mefisto had not predicted they would, and their departure was consequently imperceptible in the days that followed—until I made a third trip to Washington Square looking for my old friends. I was in a very different mood for that one. I arrived at the arch before I realized I had not taken a taxi. I had walked, but I was sadder then than I had ever been.

I am making a jumble of this narrative. I am an old man; it is a matter of course that I will jump ahead and come back and expect you to know at all times where we're at. It's not narrative guile; old age and anxiety, that's all it is. Still, while I am jumping around I might as well tell you something else out of sequence, so I cannot be accused of playing the suspense game.

At about the time I discovered my aches and pains were on the run, I kept an appointment with my Deere doctor. He insisted on examining me at frequent intervals to check on my cell count, to see if they and my platelets fell below a certain level. Though God knows what he and Hamilton could do after their DS diagnosis.

Wave good-bye to my disappearing cells? This time he had his technician do the red-cell test there in the office. He returned to the examining room with a curious look, as if I were presenting him with a new problem. He said, "There is a rise, a very slight rise but a rise in your red cells. Call me tomorrow after the lab report comes in and we'll see about the others."

I asked, "Is that good?" although I knew; I wanted to sound debonair about my fate. Ha-ha.

When he nodded and said, "Any rise is good," I did not tell him about the injections, of course. This was a pact between me and Mefisto. A secret love affair, and it had already begun to pay off.

Love Affair number 2: In the real world where Gwendolyn dwelt. But my joy in that—my declaration—took place before my cells started asserting themselves. I went straight downstairs and there was a taxi right at the end of the canopy. It left me at the arch in Washington Square Park, and right beyond it sat both Old Gents, on the first bench of those that circled the center oval which once was a spouting fountain, sometimes an ice rink and now an open-air theater in the round for aspiring stand-up comics and acrobats in danger of busting their cranium on its brick, slanting pavement. With a spurt of energy I could not ordinarily muster, I went straight to them.

"You know each other!" I exclaimed.

The dour Washington Heights fellow looked at his watch and said, "A full half-hour."

The Italian from Bleecker Street was delighted by that. He smiled and nodded. We gave each other our names. I started it, and then Joe Rivera announced his as if it were an illness, and the other said, "Marc Grassi," as if he'd take it back if we had any objections.

I asked Marc, "Did you doctor change your heart medicines?"

Joe gave Marc a distrustful look. "You said that was three weeks ago."

Marc nodded as if to an immutable fact of life.

"That's how long..." I said. "I hardly been out." I sat down at the end of the bench on Joe's side.

Marc said, "Not a setback, I hope."

"No, actually something good," I began. Do I dare tell them about Gwendolyn? "But tell me about your medicines. You know, I was here the following Thursday."

"I told him already," Marc said, nodding towards Joe.

"Go ahead," Joe said.

"He took me off the diuretic, but my ankles started to swell. So he put me back on half the amount. That's what I take now."

Joe said, "I say absolutely no salt instead, no salt whatsoever."

Marc lifted an ankle to one knee. "That takes a saint from the old country. Look. Pretty slim, huh?" He looked from Joe to me. "Huh?"

Joe shrugged. "No salt is better."

Marc said, "Remember how we used to say about girls, she's got the slimmest ankles in Manhattan?"

Joe inhaled and exhaled eloquently.

After a moment, during which I debated with myself, Marc looked across Joe at me and got my attention. He said, "What was that something good you mentioned?"

"I'm in love," I said. I had dared track down Mefisto: I could talk to them about love. It's a fallacy that men don't talk about love. Men talk about everything.

They looked at me as if I had said what I said. Joe frowned with the hope that he could convince me that some obligation had just come to mind, and he must now leave. Marc rubbed the ankle he had lifted for show and used the other hand to lower it to the ground. They were embarrassed. Of course. But not because they would not talk about love, but because they had a lifetime's practice of avoiding New York nuts and they had gone and made a mistake with me.

"I mean it," I said. "It's true."

Joe placed his hands on each side of his hams, preparatory to pulling himself out of his seat. "Well, my time has come..."

"I'm in love with this young girl," I insisted, and at the word "young" Joe gave me a strong look. I went on, "She's in love with me, too. You're the only people I've told. It just happened on the phone, and I am feeling so good I had to tell somebody who's not a kid of mine or some old lady..."

Joe said, "What happened on the phone?" and waited: if I replied sanely, he might stay.

"Conversation," I said. "I'm not crazy. She told me she loved me and I told her I love her."

In a low voice, after looking around, Marc asked, "You can still function?"

I was sure Mefisto was going to bring that back, too, so I said, "Yes," but not assertively.

"Congratulations," Joe said, but he still kept an eye to catch me out or, in any case, to emphasize his skepticism. "I can't give you any advice about that anymore. How about you, Marc?"

Marc giggled. I was sure he giggled like that forty years ago.

"I knew you'd be the ones who'd understand," I said. "Isn't that great!" I had not been so at ease with anyone in a long time. Not since the war had I had buddies like them. "Something told me one of you might be here. Isn't it great!"

"I already said congratulations," Joe said.

Marc checked the nearby benches again but kept his voice low anyway. "I think you oughta ask your doctor."

Joe said, "I never believed that stuff about guys dropping dead while in the saddle."

It was difficult for Marc to insist on anything, but he tackled the subject again. "My doctor asked me if I was sexually active, you know. If I said yes, I think he was gonna change my medicines."

"Oh, the hell with doctors," Joe said. "Let me know when the two of you get off the phone."

Marc said, "I never talked to my friend here on the phone..."

Joe lifted a hand that stopped him. "I mean him and his girlfriend. I wanna hear what happens when they get off the phone."

It was my turn to giggle. "It's like we're fifteen again, really, think about it."

"Fifteen!" Marc involuntarily exclaimed. He shook his head. "You mean it? You did it at fifteen!"

Joe remained calm. "At fifteen we were just boasting." So he was not leaving, and I could tell he didn't mind if the conversation continued on this track. "I sure was."

There was no question Marc was enjoying himself, shy though he is. "She told you first, right?" he said. "Then you told her."

I nodded a couple of times, bobbing my head like a kid. "Right, right," I said.

Joe did not get it. "What does it matter, who said what first?"

Marc threw out his arms to the sides, a gesture of surrender, but after a shake or two of the head, said, "It matters. Shows our friend is a gentlemen, not aggressive. You know what I mean."

"He shoulda kept quiet," Joe said. He fixed his eyes on me without let-up. He hoped to at least make me fidget, but I did not. Then with that same solemn stare, he slowly winked.

"Next time," I said, and waited for both to look at me, "I wanna take you to lunch."

They stared at me as if I had turned into a stranger.

"To celebrate," I explained.

Marc looked at Joe. Joe looked at the fountain again.

"Come on," I said. "It's no big deal. We'll go to some place around here."

Marc was the first to give in. "Okay, but no Italian," he said. "You know how much pasta this belly has processed!"

Joe shrugged. "There's a genuine Spanish restaurant over there on Thompson, but I never been."

"That's it," I said. "We'll go there."

"Listen, I gotta tell you," Joe said. "I won't..."

"I'm paying," I said. "I invited."

"Yeah, but I can't return the compliment," he said. I could see Marc on the other side of him writhing with—I hate to use the word—compassion.

"I don't want any compliments," I said quick. I was not going to allow Joe to turn me into an upper-middle-class type, alien to them, and it was a pleasure to see how my reply got Marc out of his suffering. He laughed with such gurgling abandon that Joe softened up.

Neither asked about Gwendolyn. Maybe to them she was just a dame, but I doubt it. To use Marc's standards, they were gentlemen. Probably by the time we met again they would have mulled over the whole of my experience and then the questions would come, plentiful and eager. We were friends, weren't we?

◇

I did learn that Tony went to the Hotel Pierre. Not outright but by indirection. He called me the day after we had lunch. It was early afternoon, and I had just returned from my second visit to the Rumanian Water Works. The wonder of this last, coming after my loving talk with my darling Gwendolyn, my encounter with my old gent friends in the park, even my painless visit to the movies with Billie Gladiola—all this had caused me to forget Tony's unhappiness. I should have called him, urged him to unburden himself. But no, that was not a style that would work with Tony, no more than it would have with me. Confessionals are tacky. However, maybe now everything was different: I was punchy with love. Was Tony? For, of course, I believed his stop at the Hotel Pierre signified he was in love.

"I don't feel I really found out how you are," he said immediately. "Yesterday, that is. I am used to seeing right through you. And you were a bit opaque."

"Funny, that's the way I felt about you," I replied, taking a stab in semi-darkness myself.

"Ah, yes," he replied in a light tone that distanced him from his words. He sighed, or I think he sighed; I heard nothing. "Did you like that wine I ordered?"

"Ah, yes," I said.

"I am thankful you're clever, Dad," he said. "It's good for me not to get away with anything."

"Ah, yes," I said. Like all repetitions, this one did not work. It didn't sound witty, but I could think of nothing else to say that was not tacky in his books.

"I think I may have been unjust about my brothers," he said. "I remember how we talked about you when we were brats, and we all idolized you. I also idolized them." I think he sighed again; he was feeling his way around. "They're all right, aren't they? They sounded fine."

Aha. He had been sent on a mission with insufficient orders. "Oh, yes, they're happy enough," I said.

"How can people be happy," he said, "when I'm sad?"

"Don't do that," I said, but that sounded ambiguous, so I added, "Be happy."

"Really?" he said.

"You can't help sadness," I advised, "but you can help happiness."

"I will," he said. "I'm a bit of a humbug—I am having fun. Sometimes. But you're right, anyway. I wanted it from the horse's mouth and you obliged."

"I'm always right," I said. "I'm your father."

"Okay," he said, and he made that coarse word sound elegant. "So much for me and my newfound Celtic moral streak, but are you *all* right?" A pause for the segue. "I've already made one slip, I might as well hold nothing back—my brothers called to enlist me in this...this...health care program. Randy is very worried, Manny, too, but not with the fine frenzy of our middle sibling."

"I'm fine..."

"Among the three of us there is enough money, and we know enough doctors and surgical specialists who perform hair-raising procedures and their clinics and rest homes. We know physical therapists who can bring you back from the dead and psychological therapists who can teach you to adjust happily to anything. If any or all of these things do not do the job, Manny and I have a rather wide knowledge of good wines and either we or our friends have enough in our cellars to keep you mellow for many years."

"A beautiful speech," I said. I was happy and mellow, I could feel that magic fluid spreading through my system like a warming wine. Tony's concern for me now was pure gravy. "I am fine, my boy. I'll make that a sentimental declaration and call you my son. I have decided to live forever."

He liked that. He reserved for it his most intimate tone. "How do you do that? Teach me."

"You make a pact with Modern Science. All I lack now is a grandchild who can play a few flourishes on a trumpet. Ta-ra-rah, here comes Germán Morán who will not die until the day the proletariat are in power throughout the entire world."

"Careful, Dad," he said. "It might happen."

◇

Again, I saw no one but Mefisto in Nine West Low. He opened the same door in the white wall. This time there was a white wire tray on the table. Three or four neat small packages sat demurely in one corner of it. He had been sure of my coming: just that unobtrusive little tray, no steaming pots in which hypodermic syringes boiled, but it was enough. He nodded and sat down. "You stand in front of me," he said. "Turn around, lower your pants in back." I hooked my thumbs into them and my undershorts, and he added, "Only just enough," I stopped my trousers halfway down and waited like an owl for the sunset. The magic fluids were extracted from their vials and drawn together in the syringe, then expelled into a vial which Mefisto held between his hands and rolled back and forth, first slowly, briskly after three or four rolls. He held it up and studied it a second, as one might a good cognac. In his other hand, he held the hypodermic, its needle pointing at the ceiling ready to fill it with the fluid once more. This was a rite. He did not once look up at me; I was free to keep my head half-turned and to watch. Keen though I was, I did not feel the actual injection. He tapped the spot with what must have been a small alcohol rub; I never saw it, only felt the moisture which evaporated before I pulled up my pants. At home, I stood before the dressing mirror and twisted and turned but could not localize the spot where the elixir of life had entered.

◇

It was a couple of days later—my body is clicking in better every day, but my mind is flying apart. It occurred to me that the advice I gave Tony was one I myself cannot follow. He does quite well on his own in maintaining a fine balance. I have lectured myself endlessly, but equanimity has eluded me all my life. I never manage a calm exterior. I try, but I cannot kid anyone. Not even my kids. Ha-ha.

Soon enough Manuel and Tony will see that I am as well physically as an old man can be, and I won't have to answer suspicious questions about my health. (Mefisto will remain my secret passionate affair.) They will recall that Randy tends always to be an alarmist. He takes things up with passion and drops them soon thereafter without learning to go easy the next time. Like me. It is extraordinary how each child appropriates some vital part of you. Randy, my instability and inattention; Manuel, my devotion to literature; Tony, my sensibility. Had there been a fourth, what would have been left for him? My common sense?

I had only just finished talking to Tony the second time when I opened my door and placed next to it a pile of the *Times* and a plastic bag filled with garbage to be picked up by the handyman, and heard myself called *Dad* again. It was Thom. I was glad to see him, even as I recalled that he is gay. He was walking Owen up and down the hall, singing *Here we go round the mulberry bush* while encouraging him to skip and hop with him. I said quite friendly, “What’s doing?” and he walked the child right into my apartment.

Owen pointed at a Zuni cow sitting on a side table and went as straight as he could towards it. “That, that,” he kept saying. As he progressed, Thom, who was standing close to me, looked up into my face with an exalted look and slid an arm around my waist. “I love you, Dad,” he murmured. “You might as well know it.”

“Excuse me,” I said, and reached the museum copy of the funny, fragile cow before Owen did. “Let me show it to you, Owen. This is a cow. Do you know what a cow is?” Never have I acted this coy, not ever. Not even with my own grandchildren, but I had to get away from Thom.

He followed me, however, and sat on the arm of the easy chair I had taken. He whispered in my ear as I leaned down to Owen. “Did you hear what I said? I love you, Dad.” One hand touched me above the elbow.

I looked up at the top of the low bookcase against the near wall where three pre-Colombian figures stood. I nodded towards them, and said, “I guess this is not a good place for children. He can reach everything.”

“I love you,” he repeated.

"That's the style these days. Everyone says *love ya* as farewell and greeting and in-between. Even my sons say it, and I know they don't mean it."

Sometimes when I am cornered I am as inventive as writers are expected to be.

"They mean it," he said, "and so do I."

He was so close to me he had only to pucker his lips for them to buss my cheek.

"Thom, I'm worried Owen is gonna smash something," I said, speaking in as low a register as I could. But I knew that no matter how manly my behavior nor how deep my voice swooped, no diversion was going to work with him. He was as determined in his way as Billie Gladiola. "He needs some attention."

"Okay." He chuckled. "Let's take him to Washington Square—how's that?"

"Washington Square?" I said as if pondering an abstract philosophical problem. Maybe I was. God knows about what. I felt light-headed enough to speculate whether I was getting enough oxygen. Going to the park might be just as hazardous as the mined territory of my living room. Then I thought of another reason to go along: it would be a couple of hours before the West Coast had been awake long enough to start making phone calls. As I said, I always come down to earth. Thom is a nice kid. Anyway, he's not going to rape me. Ha-ha. By the time I thought this thought I was already at the door. I opened it quickly.

Thom went past me with a smile. He winked and thus let me know he could tell what was going on in my mind. I had to smile back: I'm not a totally humorless fellow once I am out of danger.

I am doing this for my Darling Gwendolyn, I said to myself a couple of times on the walk to Washington Square as if singing a Song, and the Magic Fluid makes it possible—capitalizing like the crazy Germans. Was it Romanticism or Mefisto? Writers have a duty to pursue asides, but I shall cut mine short and tell you that in sight of the arch I thought of the Old Gents. This was not a Thursday, but what was to keep them from being there? I thought of the possibility fearfully—then mischievously. What will they think of Thom; what will he think of them? A dark suspicion flew into my mind, and I gave Thom a sharp look.

Thom is a good caretaker. Responsible, too. He walked along with Owen holding his hand and directing almost every word to him. Nothing he said to me was compromising, thank God. I don't like scenes out in the street, only at home—ha-ha! We made a rather typical three-generations family group, and I calmed down enough to pursue asides, such as the matter of capitalization. We used to do it, too, but in the eighteenth century. I was amused at myself: when I have no real knowledge, I dump my observations into the eighteenth century. Anyway, who is that *we*? We Wasps? *There*'s another capitalization.

The Old Gents were not there, which was just as well. What could I say to them? How to phrase it? *Thom here is a nice fairy*. Or had they progressed to *faggot*? No, they were gentlemen.

Thom took the walk bordering the dog run. He headed for a bench there which would be all ours. "You like the day, don't you?" he said to me. To Owen, "See the dogs? We love them but we don't touch them. Agreed?"

He gave me a very suggestive look when he said *touch*. That is, he lifted his eyebrows and blinked fast. I had to laugh.

Owen was in stasis. He understood, but he did not want to say yes. Instead, he headed for the bench across from ours, where a boy his age was staring at him, and Thom got up and followed him. The boy's mother appeared to welcome the two of them. She was black-haired, looked up with round Little Orphan Annie eyes, and drew back rather good legs. Thom and she exchanged some words, and in a while (I was not watching) he drifted back to me. He said, looking back at her, "She'll keep an eye on both."

He sat down on our bench, and said in a voice that would not carry, "She thinks you're my father."

I looked at her again, and she half-waved and grinned. I nodded. "Naturally," I said to him.

"I want you to be my Dad," he said, "even if it's not natural. There's nothing really natural in this world, really."

I was not going to argue.

"You like Gwennie, don't you?"

I said, "Stop talking nonsense," but not harshly.

"I know, you're gonna say that's the way you're made and if you're nice, and I know you're nice, you're gonna say that's the way I'm made and never the twain..."

"That's nonsense. I'm not about to say any of those things," I said, myself again. "In fact, I was not about to say anything, my boy."

I looked up and down the walk and saw that Owen and the other boy leaned against the chicken wire of the dog run and both were peaceable.

"No one can hear me," Thom said. "I've had theater training."

I leaned back and stretched my legs and noticed that my tendons did not ache as a result.

"Actually, I'm glad you're the way...you are. I don't want you to be like Stacey."

He stopped and waited.

I obliged him: "How's that?"

"Accommodating..." He chuckled. "Caught ya!"

I had forgotten all about Stacey and the student movie. "How is he?" I asked.

"I'm telling you, accommodating," he repeated, but with a slight frown this time. "He's an actor."

"How's he doing on that movie?" I said. "I forgot about that."

"He's getting along," he said, "accommodating all the way down the line."

I must admit I was a bit tickled by his conversation, but I really did not want to be part of it. I should prefer to overhear it. Anyway, being with him was not of any help to Gwendolyn. I must get away. But why? It was still too early for the West Coast.

Thom sprang up and went over to Owen and his playmate. I heard the girl say, "They're fine, fine. I'll call you if..." But anyone could tell she would prefer if he stayed and chatted with her.

He returned. "The reason I'm glad you're not like Stacey is—here goes—when you let me take care of you someday—I said *some*day, not today—where was I? Yes, I'll know then there will be some real feeling involved."

I was taken aback—if anything can appear untoward anymore—but I quickly saw it differently. His judgment on promiscuity was smart of him. He was a good kid, but I had to tell him, "There's nothing to take care of."

My talking to the point seemed to buoy him. I was acting rather nice myself: instead of rejecting his extraordinary and mildly disquieting offer, I told him I couldn't deliver. Why hurt his feelings?

"When I take care of you, Dad," he said, and paused, not because he was shy or was checking the other benches, but out of feeling for me. He dared it anyway. "When I do it, you'll get hard."

Time to go, no reason to hang around. I looked at my watch; it was nine a.m. in L.A. I placed a hand on each knee to push myself to my feet. Thom reached out and held my elbow. "Don't go. I know you have real values—I finished *Jack* last night. I can tell, you couldn't get that bastard down so perfectly if you weren't just the opposite. I really respect you as an artist. As anything, really. You know what I mean?"

"You liked *Jack*, huh?" I said, and stayed.

◇

A good thing I stayed. I did not know then that I would look back on this day as the happiest in the whole affair. We ambled back to our building while he criticized the theater world the way I do publishing. Not as bitterly, to tell the truth, for his tone was happy with the sense that his critique was an insight which would stand him in good stead in his career. Not mine: I expected never to publish again, but nevertheless I was happy, more or less, because of Gwendolyn and Mefisto and my three sons who worried about my well-being. I ambled up Fifth alongside Thom and Owen, and was so full of well-being that I was ready to throw an arm around Thom's shoulders, but did not for fear he might take it seriously.

When we parted on our floor, Thom said, "You're right to like Gwennie—she's great."

Yes, I said to myself, and went inside and looked for the red blinking light on my answering machine from the instant I opened the door and could peek to the right and see it from there. There were no messages. I stepped farther in, closed the door behind me and said to myself, There's something wrong. How many days has it been? Three? Four? Mefisto's Magic Fluid had addled me about that. And Randy, why hasn't he called either? I groaned aloud.

I have been living in a fool's paradise, I said to myself, and cursed that I should express my anguish with such a lousy cliché. The two of them did get together. I knew it as I stared at the answering machine. That's why I had not heard from either. Or they shacked up with a couple of others. This last possibility was more attractive, less of a betrayal. What did I care with whom Randy slept? And for Gwendolyn it was only a temporary measure, not a betrayal at all. Well, almost not. I sat down in front of the phone and breathed evenly. I had taken my emotional temperature, and I was not running a fever. Well, then why had neither called me?

The phone rang, of course.

"Sweetheart, you're there!" she exclaimed. "I got it!"

"What? What?" I said.

"Of course, you don't know!" She continued without drawing breath. "I didn't tell you on purpose. I read for a feature film for PBS. Oh, the suspense! The youngest of the three—I got it!"

"What? What?" I felt condemned to this interpolation.

"Chekov's! Chekov's! Darling sweetheart! An oil company is giving a small fortune to PBS, but only to do *The Three Sisters*. I think they wanted to use the money for something else—I'm glad, glad!" She let out her breath. "Ooh..."

"Congratulations," I said. "You'll be perfect."

"I owe it all to you," she said. "You introduced me to Randy."

"Randy?" I said.

"Didn't he tell you?" she said.

She waited a moment, but I was speculating about too many things to reply.

"That very first evening—after I talked to you, remember?—I was having dinner out with a friend and Randy came in with Dawn Ippolito. Sorry, you know who Dawn Ippolito is? I don't mean to drop names."

I said, "Everybody knows Dawn Ippolito is Riverview Studios," which is no more than she deserved.

"Over here she stops traffic. So-o-oh, he stopped by our table and told me I should give him a call, that he had run into the casting person out there filming auditions for the project. I mean, *Three Sisters*. Isn't that funny: I come all the way here for a New York audition! So I called him the moment I got back home—here, I mean."

And thus my beautiful day came to an end.

But not Gwendolyn. "And the big audition my agent set up for me is too terrible to mention. It was for a pilot for a sitcom—I guess you know what that is, too. I could not believe how gross it is. Totally mindless. I look at the so-called script and say to myself, What am I going to do? So I did nothing, I just sailed through without one thought for—I'm talking too much. Whoosh!"

"No," I said weakly. "I'm interested."

"So-o-oh, I'm the number-one candidate. They keep calling my agent—they just did. One more person has to see me and agree. And then I have to sign a contract. It's not only terrible, but I have a real out: you have to sign up for five years if the pilot succeeds. Five years! And in the secondary, little-sister role! My agent just has to understand. Everyone says they'd understand a reason like that, but an artistic one—never."

I took a chance. "What does Randy think?"

It was her turn to say, "Randy?"

"Aren't you seeing him?"

"Actually, as a matter of fact, tonight is his last night and there's something arranged..."

"And that includes Dawn Ippolito?"

"Sweetheart, you're clairvoyant! But she doesn't bother even looking at actors. She has casting directors for that."

"And so Randy is returning tomorrow?" I said. "I thought he was already back."

"Actually, he might stay longer," she said. "I don't really know. He has something cooking with Dawn. Shall I tell him when I see him tonight that you were asking about him. I'll do that."

It says something about our times that our lives' denouements happen on the phone, not to speak of minor climaxes. No one visits, no one writes letters. There are no clinches and no fisticuffs, only long distance calls and shoot-outs.

"But I called to find out about you!" she said. "You must not think, sweetheart, that I'm this self-centered all the time. I love you."

What the hell, I'll ask her where she's staying.

She whispered, "I'm really calling to hear you say you love me."

After a while, I said, "Let's move on to other things. Where're you staying?"

"I believe—I really do—that is what did it," she said in a voice that started deep in her throat. "That's what brought me all this luck: your telling me you love me." Then, in a sober key: "I hope you'll sit down with me and tell me about Chekov."

"Not much to say," I replied. "I never met him."

"You rogue."

"Why don't you give me your number," I said, "and I'll call you as soon as I get something out of the way... and we'll talk Chekov as long as you like."

"Oh, no, I want to face you when we sit and talk about him," she said. "I'll ask you to read some of the lines. The phone is so inadequate for all that."

I gave up. I placed my elbows on the desk and covered my face with my hands; but I am too old and dehydrated to cry. The damned phone gives the date and the time, and only five minutes went by before it rang.

I said into it, "Hello, Randy, call back in fifteen minutes."

"You guessed..." he began, but I didn't let him finish. I hung up.

In the old days it took me less than five to shower. I was putting on my bathrobe and was leaving the bathroom when the phone rang again. He did not wait the full fifteen minutes.

"Dad!" he said. "Are you all right?"

"How're you doing with Dawn Ippolito?"

"How'd you know I've been busy with her?" he asked.

"Didn't Gwendolyn Costello tell you?" I said, sure she shared his hotel room. "I talked to her today. Let's see, exactly twenty minutes ago."

"That's right," he said. "They met."

"So, how's Dawn?"

"Dad, don't be so suspicious," he said, obviously relieved I was on the wrong track. "She's gay."

I said, "I'm sure you won't hold that against her."

"Dad, if I told anyone my father talked like this to me, no one would believe me," he said proudly. "So tell me, how are you."

"Fine," I said. "I so informed both your brothers."

"Dad, I have to share my concerns with my brothers," he said. "Especially when I'm going to be away. They would never forgive me. They count on me. I confess I also called them after they saw you. They reported you are in fine fettle."

He made a small dent in my anger and anxiety. "Okay," I said. "But I'm the best authority on how I'm feeling."

"Let me tell you about Dawn Ippolito," he said, happily changing to the key of Success Major. "I've stayed this long because she wants us to work out a story line before I begin writing the script. That's why we're having dinner tonight. If everything goes right..."

"What?" I said impatiently.

"If we're both happy with the third-act idea I'll give her, then I'll come back tomorrow. This is a very hard-working town, contrary to what everyone thinks."

"What's Gwendolyn Costello got to do with your third act? Whatever that is," I said.

"I ran into her at Sound Stage, and I've introduced her to a couple of people. I don't want to brag," he said. "And Dawn Ippolito is very big time. That's why I asked her to join us tonight."

"Is that so," I said as flatly as it was possible for me at that moment.

"She's at a point in her career when she needs to network," he explained.

My reply burst out of me. I never planned it. "I love that girl! Watch out how you act with her."

"Dad, that's very sweet of you," he said. "Really nice that you're taking an interest, so generous..."

"Cut it out," I said. "Don't do that to me."

"Dad, I know you're not good at receiving compliments," he said, and took on a confessional semi-guilty tone. "And Sheila has never encouraged you to be close with us. The longer I'm married to her the more...but never mind that. It's wonderful for Gwennie that she can count on you."

I interrupted, determined to make him understand. "Randy, she loves me..."

"Of course, I always knew you were a sentimental guy under all that crust. Let's face it...you're..."

"She loves me, you understand!" I yelled.

"I know, she told me," he replied. "Her own father drank himself to death, life was a blur, he never noticed his children. And I told Gwennie that your daughters-in-law are all too self-centered..."

I hung up on him. When the phone rang again, I heard him say, "The operator cut us..." and I picked it up and hung up without putting the receiver to my ear.

What am I going to do now?

I turned off the answering machine. I let the phone ring. I did not pick it up. I lay on my bed and tried to think it through. I had to resolve it; I could not go on this way if I was going to live forever. Of course, Randy was right to take the tack he did. And Gwendolyn could not mean to be more than a nineteenth-century loving daughter to her substitute father. So what did that leave me? Thom, I guess. I still had the wit to laugh soundlessly at that, then felt somewhat sorry I did not grant poor Thom leave to be anguished. I finally answered the phone when it next rang a couple of hours later. It was Billie Gladiola. Ha-ha.

"Gerry, even my husband never got this many calls from me," she said right off, "but there's a spate of movies my friends disapprove of and you never talk about literature, thank God."

"Okay, when?" I said

"In three days," she said. "This time I pay. This is no boyfriend-girlfriend date, you know."

"I'll pay for the popcorn," I said.

"I guess you're not going to the memorial for Clarence Schlumberger tonight," she said.

"He was just a talkative socialist," I said.

"I'm going," she said in her serious voice. "He kept the faith."

"I like the ones who throw bombs," I said.

"Threw," she said. "No one throws bombs anymore."

"Down in Chiapas they do," I said.

That was bound to keep her quiet for three days. I did not glory in my put-down. I thought about the phenomenon of Billie Gladiola for the next ten minutes or so, and decided that she was okay. Maybe not those broads who followed her about. If I was gonna be around for so long, I should find better targets for my sniping. God, I hope I am not going to turn into a reasonable man.

Aiee, aiee, aiee. I held a wake for myself that night. And the following one. And on the third day I answered the phone. It was Billie Gladiola.

"Can we make it next week?" she said.

"If I don't die in the meanwhile," I said.

"Don't do that. I'd have to go to another memorial," she said, "and give another talk."

I said lugubriously, "I'm gonna live forever."

"Okay," she said, "today there's this thing at the United Nations."

"Are you gonna be inside sipping martinis or outside picketing?"

"Cut it out," she said.

"So it's inside," I said. "How do you feel welcoming all those victims of socialism to Farrar Straus, et cetera?"

"Is this a shakedown?" she said. "You wanna be paid to keep quiet?"

I laughed.

She snapped her gum, and we agreed about next week. An hour later I was depressed again. But perhaps not as much. I had more energy to pick up the phone when it rang again.

It was Manny. "Dad, you're making Randy nervous again. He says you hung up on him, but really that's not what I'm calling about."

I said, "I suppose Randy thinks I've got to be sick to hang up on him."

"He well may," Manny said. "But this time he thinks you're disgusted with him because he's having an affair."

"He's having an affair?"

"Of course," Manny said, a bit patronizingly. "He's always having an affair and he tells me about them because he believes I have the psychological acumen to understand the healthy role they play in his life."

"And you do?" I said.

"Of course," he said. "I wanted to ask you what you know about the final days in Madrid. There was street fighting? Is that so? Even after the Popular Front government gave in?"

"Yes," I said.

"It's not been written up much," he said. "And to have been there, to have lived through it after three years of...that must have been the low point of the century, it seems to me, and yet no one's written about it."

"Because it was the Communists who called for resistance to the end," I said.

"Yes?" he said when I stopped.

"You're not supposed to say anything nice about Communists," I said. I stopped again because I did not want to sound like Billie Gladiola. "You're supposed to call them Stalinists and let it go at that."

"Hmmm," he murmured. He audibly inhaled. "Listen, Sylvie is trying to pin down a day when we can have you to dinner."

"Tell her not to bother," I said. "She'll only cancel it the morning of."

"And don't worry about Randy. As he says, L.A. puts him in a ravishment mood," he said lightly, too amused to argue about Sylvie. "He's writing a script for a big producer, bagged a name director for his lecture series and a couple of stars..."

"Yes, yes, I'm sure," I said.

"Dad, it's very moving, what happened in Spain," he said. "It breaks your heart to read about it."

After he hung up, I decided it was he who is most like me. I thought about what he said—not the Spain part: I could not bear to think about that anymore—and became depressed again. I could not bear the part about Randy and his ravishments either, but the vision of my darling Gwendolyn was insistent. It would not leave me alone.

I did not go out for another day. Again, I ordered in a meal from the Chinese restaurant. But I did go down for the mail, and when I got back, there was a message on the machine from Tony. "This is to tell you I got a call from Randy, but I'm not worrying," he said in his beguiling voice. "I'm not a serious person, that's why." There was a pause during which the machine's tape crackled and shrieked. "I hope you don't want me to be a serious person." A very slight pause, and he added, "Dad."

I decided he was the most like me.

◇

Each day I took fewer painkillers. I bent down to pick up objects I dropped with less effort each time. My spirits did not respond to my material well-being, to put it the way an old Red like me should have. I got a call from Deere's secretary, an excessively efficient young woman, to urge me, if I were in the neighborhood, to drop in any time to have a blood sample taken. I did so, and when my Deere doctor saw me, he said he was curious merely—nothing to worry about—and asked me to wait in the examining room to get the result of the red-cell count. He returned and said, "They're up again, so were the lab results last week on the others. We must be doing something right." I nodded at him but did not tell him about the Rumanian Water Works. It was not my job to go around enlightening people.

I did not go out again until the day for my lunch date with my old friends. I did not receive any other calls, except sales pitches (which I welcome because it allows me to yell guiltlessly) and I did not phone anyone. Not even to check if Randy was back. If he were not home, his wife would panic at the thought that she should invite me over. In fact, the only persons I wanted to be with were Joe and Marc. I looked out the windows to see what people were wearing, and decided a flannel shirt and a sober Brooks jacket would be fine. When I opened my door, I thought of Owen and Thom but had no time to wonder about them, for coming out into the hall simultaneously was Gwendolyn. She was alone and prettily dressed to go out and as surprised as the perennial deer in the car's headlights.

"Gwendolyn!" I exclaimed hoarsely, and all the hurt and good feeling rushed back into my chest. I held out an arm, then pulled it back. I meant to say more but could not.

"Sweetheart!" She extended both arms, wide and generously, as she half ran towards me. Like the last take in a lousy movie, I thought bitterly. Nevertheless, she hugged me and tilted her head back and genuinely smiled and locked her eyes into mine: I was lost and out of control. I pulled her body to me, joined our pelvises and brought my head down to kiss her. She did not resist but neither did she encourage me as in the past, holding her head in such a way that my kiss landed on her chin and placing a hand on my chest to keep me distant.

"I got here this morning on the Red Eye!" she said. "And have to go straight to the reading and I'm a wreck. How do I look?"

◇

"Child, darling girl!" I said, and brought my tense, wild hands to her breasts. "I want you."

She looked round and beyond me—of course, we were out in the hall. I didn't care; I tried again to kiss her lips. The elevator door opened and brushed against me. I had to step back away from Gwendolyn.

She was quick to say, "Are you going down, too?" but she did not quite manage to change the aspect of the scene that greeted Ernestine Puglia. She walked past me, with a murmured *Excuse me* as if she had other business on this floor than to knock on my door. I could not have spoken to her if I wanted. Gwendolyn held the door open and said, "Coming?" with a brave look.

"Yes." It sounded like a gasp. I followed her into the elevator, and there I tried again, less violently this time.

It did not work. She turned to watch the door close as I reached for her, and I saw she was afraid. She talked fast. "I had to leave suddenly or lose my chance at *Three Sisters*—they could still get out of it. I wanted to approach it differently. I wanted to listen to you about Chekov's characters . . . you know so much and so deeply."

She could tell the crisis was over and looked back over her shoulder at me and smiled as she spoke. The air had been let out of me. She said just before the old elevator slowed down for the lobby, "But Randy was on the plane last night and I got...you didn't know?"

I patted her cheek. "Yes," I said.

"A chance to pick his brains about Chekov," she continued. "He's very knowledgeable. He must've gotten it from you." With that she walked ahead of me into the lobby. She stopped a moment and in this way kept me from proceeding to the front door of our building. "Still, it's you I wanted. Your understanding...you see?"

I should have held back and allowed her to leave without me, but I followed her, yearning but without hope. At the end of the canopy stood Randy, a taxi beyond him with its back door open. He was speaking towards it when we came out, and thus when he turned he was unprepared to see me.

"Dad!" He quickly glanced at Gwendolyn. No help there. He lied: "I called you, but your phone was busy."

He put an arm around me and patted my back in the Spanish fashion. "I have so much to tell you. What a time it's been. If you only knew." He laughed falsely at his own locution. "You will, you will."

I did not feel or think anything.

"I'm dropping off Gwennie at her appointment midtown," he said. "Can I take you wherever?"

That stirred me: what could be worse than a ride with the two of them. I shook my head a couple of times.

"No?" he said, relieved. "Did Manny and Tony keep in touch?"

I said nothing.

"Oh, you and I already talked about that," he said, not the least bit embarrassed.

"Sweetheart?" Gwendolyn called from the taxi and waved at me.

"What say?" Randy asked again, gladly now that he knew I would say no. "Coming with us?"

I shook my head. "No, no, I'm going the other way," I said, and turned to walk down the street in the direction the taxi could not go.

My back was to them when Randy called out, "Dad, see you soon, okay?"

I kept walking, propelled only by the Magic Fluid. When I heard the taxi take off, I leaned against a wild pear tree at the edge of the sidewalk. I looked down as if I were studying the little bronze plaque that said it had been planted there in memory of Amy Rose Ottoway. It was Gwendolyn's body which occupied me, her peaked small breasts, how her groin felt against me. Nothing had happened to mine. There was no one coming up the sidewalk, so I allowed myself a groan. I was in command again: I could moan or not; it was my decision.

◇

Joe Rivera got to Washington Square Park ahead of me and sat at the first bench beyond the arch. I could see him as I waited for the light to change. I had already decided that I was much too alarmed about Gwendolyn's trip to L.A., and the sight of Joe helped lift my spirits even more.

Joe wore a tie and a white shirt, and I acted as if I didn't notice. I used to wear three-piece Brooks suits like Norman Mailer, but no more. Still, I was no slob, and I did not shame Joe when I showed up. He got up and shook hands, and then we sat down and looked around. No Marc Grassi.

Joe said, "That Marc lives around here, right?"

A half-hour later we had already pooled our knowledge of Marc's illnesses, symptoms, the medicines he takes. We stayed at the bench and did not walk the paths radiating from the central fountain behind the arch. Grassi could not get lost here.

Another half-hour, and Joe pressed his lips and nodded. "You hungry?" he said.

"Absolutely," I said. "Let's go."

I knew where we were heading, but it was only polite to act as if he was showing me. As we crossed into the narrow streets below the park, I said, "Maybe he'll show up next week."

As if to put a stop to that kind of talk, Joe said, "It's called La Parilla."

I got into the spirit of it. "Sounds like it's northern Spain all right—Galician, Asturian, maybe Basque."

"Argentinians like to grill their meat outdoors, too," Joe said.

"That's 'cause of all the Galicians who emigrated there," I said. "Practically everybody there."

"That explains it," Joe said with more energy than he usually invests.

"More Gallegos in Buenos Aires than in any Galician city in Spain. I mean Santiago de Compostela, Vigo, La Coruña."

"Is that so?" he said, and smiled faintly.

That same smile reappeared when we entered La Parilla. Windows out front, but it was still dim inside. Beige and ocher; no Andalucian colors or white stucco. There were serviceable tables and chairs crowding the low-ceilinged small space arranged with no thought for passageways for customers or waiters. A small bar against half a wall, the far end opened into the kitchen. A red-faced, squat man came out of there to take a look at us. We did not alarm him, but he wasn't sure. There was a warm smell of prawns and squids, garlic and saffron.

The restaurant's only waiter looked our way, too. He was carrying dessert dishes to the few tables still occupied, and said, "*Cualquiera*," and went on to serve his customers. Joe did not bother to nod; he was going to sit where he pleased anyway.

I looked around when we sat down at a sturdy chair and wooden table. There was nothing in the place that you could say was pretty or charming or quaint, but I found it very attractive. Joe looked at home, too. A racial memory, very likely, but I did not say that to him.

He said in a low voice, "He is serving them *flan*, the real thing, not since my mother..."

"That's right, not since my mother either," I said. "I'm gonna have it."

"Me, too, when the times comes," Joe said soberly. He pointed a finger at me. "I'm helping out with this bill."

"Take it easy," I said. "I invited."

He made a noise that I recognized from the men in my hometown: it said who paid wasn't settled. Fighting for the check is a question of honor. They were all dead now, those men with old Spanish manners, and they seemed not to have passed on this gift to the younger generations.

The waiter immediately said, "Wine?"

Joe looked at me. "How are you about that?"

"What the hell," I said. "*Un día es un día.*"

The waiter winked. "I knew you were Spanish," he said, in Spanish. "I got a nice Rioja."

Joe said, "A whole bottle?"

"Remember," I said. "*Un día . . .*"

He decided to have the yellow rice and shrimps, me the squid in its dye, to phrase it the way the Spaniards do, and the waiter went off quickly to alert the cook. He came back with the wine and two plates with marinated red peppers decorated with thin slices of anchovies. "Here, play with that," he said. "Those dishes are going to take a half-hour."

Joe was once an apprentice waiter in Chelsea, but when he came back from the war, he knew that the Spanish colony there was fading, and he had learned to drive a truck, so . . . Then the Teamsters Union came in and . . . He sighed. "I guess you got grandchildren?"

I nodded. "You?"

"My son and his wife never had any kids," he said. "And I never had a pension or medical plan. I hear talk about all that. Must be a good thing."

"An income is always a good thing," I said. "Grandchildren, it depends."

"Some can turn out bad," he said.

"No, I mean it depends on the grandfather," I said. "I'm a lousy grandfather."

He liked that.

"I gotta pee," I said, and went off to the tiny men's room. Since Joe was interested in the other customers, I gave the waiter my credit card without his seeing me do it and told him not to bring a bill to the table. I figured this was a ploy that Joe would not foresee.

"Prostate, huh?" he said when I got back.

I nodded.

"Me, too," he said. "Did I tell you?"

Should I tell him about Mefisto? But at that moment our marvelous orders arrived. I told Joe about Ybor City, that I knew all these dishes from there. And from my mother, of course.

"You know, I heard about Ybor City," he said. "Also, Gary, Indiana." He paused, then added, "I don't wanna say anything, but those Dominicans, et cetera, they..."

"They sure are," I agreed.

Waves of goodness steamed up from the huge serving platters the waiter set before us. "I'll leave you alone for a long, slow tango," he said.

Joe tucked the cloth napkin in his shirt collar and smoothed it down. He took a forkful of the rice, and said, "See that yellow? That's real saffron."

I pointed to my dark, oxford-gray rice and said, "See that, that's real dye."

Ah, it was grand: this was my real life.

Joe never asked me any questions about my other life. (Not a word either about Gwendolyn after all my boasting last week: he knew how those things come and go.) I don't think he ever asked me what I did either. He was curious, I am certain, but he lived by the rules of the country people of the north. He did not intrude. They waited: if one was a genuine friend, one volunteered the details of one's life. Or they asked other people about one. One? In Joe's presence you used the impersonal pronoun. I decided to tell him about my cancer, for our friendship's sake, and about Mefisto's Magic Fluid for his. But first the flan.

"No cream cheese in this," he said after the first spoonful. He savored the slightly bitter caramelized sugar. "The real thing."

"Your mother?" I said. "She made it with no short cuts, right?"

He nodded and took a second spoonful with great care.

"Mine, too," I said. "All fresh milk."

With the *café solo*, a dark, dark espresso, I said, "You know, Joe, that prostate trouble I told you about? It's cancer."

He nodded. "It figures," he said. "You'd never been checked down there—they were too busy with your heart."

"That's right," I said.

"They don't use radiation or chemotherapy no more," he said. "They don't do much good."

"At first they told me nothing could be done for me," I said, not wishing to go into details and thus letting him know what a dope I had been, "but now I get an injection once a month."

"Lupron," he said. "It's the treatment of choice, like they say."

I stared at him. "How'd you know?"

"It's no atomic secret," he said. "It puts everything on hold until you die of something else."

The laughter which burst out of me brought the waiter out of the kitchen. "Another espresso?" he called. We had the place to ourselves now.

"Yes, yes!" I said to him.

To Joe, "You mean I won't live forever!"

The waiter said, "It's on the house," and disappeared into the kitchen again.

"You didn't know?" Joe said. "Your doctor didn't tell you about it, how it's hormonal and all that?"

"I don't think I asked," I said.

"You gotta," he said. "or they act like the practice of medicine is a big mystery."

I thought it over. "It is a big mystery," I said.

The waiter brought the free espresso. He suggested, "How about a cognac?"

"Naw, thanks," Joe said.

I said, "It would kill us."

"In that case, the moment of truth has arrived," the waiter said. The moment of truth has come, indeed, I said to myself. He reached into his white jacket pocket, gave me my credit card, placed the final bill and a ballpoint in front of me and retreated to a respectful distance.

"What's that?" Joe said, but he took out his wallet as he asked. "Remember, we split."

It took much arguing, as it would have in Ybor City in the old days, but he finally persuaded me to let him leave the tip at least. He had got a look at the bill, and I saw him flinch as he focused on the total. We got up and he removed a single dollar bill from his wallet. He placed it on the table and anchored it with the espresso cup. He walked ahead of me to the street, proud of his whole participation in the lunch.

"Wait for me," I said to him outside the door. "I gotta pee again."

Thank God, the waiter had not yet gone to our table to clear up. I added six dollars to Joe's one, so that the tip exactly totaled twice the sales tax, our formula in New York City: I'm no big tipper myself.

Outside, he was studying the curb. "I'll bet even money Marc will be here next week. What about you?"

"Sure, sure, I'll be here," I said. "Marc must've had something to take care of for his daughter today."

"Yeah, he's not very sick," he said. "We're the bad ones." He came close to smiling a totally happy smile.

The whole street, half in thin sunlight, half black shade, the kiosk spilling over with newspapers and dirty magazines, the old Italian in a long, white apron in front of his pasta shop—all of it looked different. I knew immediately what had happened to me while I was inside with Joe: I was down to earth again. No more symbols, just the facts of life smiled at me from the worn street.

Joe peered at the papers. "Just the headlines," he said. "That's enough for me."

One block up, on the corner of Fourth, Joe stopped and put out his hand. "I'm going to Sixth to take the number five," he said. He gave my hand an extra shake. "Listen, that was a good lunch."

I said, "Maybe next week we'll all be hungry again."

He turned from the middle of the street. "We split—and we go to McDonald's," he said.

He's right, I said to myself as I walked up to Washington Square in tune with my new outlook, but when I entered the park, I said, No, we gotta have our flings, too. My inner camera quickly clicked an image of Gwendolyn on and off, and I was able to smile to myself, and say, yes, yes.

Out of nowhere I heard Thom's voice call, "Dad!" I turned in its direction and figured from his smile that he had caught me mumbling to myself. He was carrying Owen. "I knocked on your door to see if you'd join us—and here you are!"

"Here I am," I repeated.

"Join me on the bench while our boy plays?"

I looked at my watch—I don't know why, I was on no schedule of any kind—and nodded. "Okay," I said. "A few minutes only."

As I accompanied Thom I realized why I looked at my watch: I wanted to be home by myself and think about the happy ordinariness of life.

Thom put Owen down and he went straight to the dog run. Soon another kid joined him at the fence. Owen taught me kids like to repeat their experiences again and again unvaryingly. He reminded me, rather. My boys used to drive me crazy reading them the same story two and three times a night. But it was Owen who also caused me to think that, actually, I was like that, too. I turned to say this to Thom, then stopped myself. It might inspire him to go into his old song and dance.

He did anyway.

I just made a face and changed the subject this time. "But why are you baby-sitting? She should be back from her audition—I know all about that."

"All?" he said. "You know all?"

"Should I?" the new me said. "Do I need to know all?"

"I'm going crazy," he said. "Gwennie tells me everything."

The old suspicions sailed right back. Who took Gwendolyn to Sound Stage the first time? Whom exactly did she stay with in L.A? Who was that Episcopalian godfather of Owen's? The new me tried to shake this creeping agony off. Go with it, as the kids say, go with it.

"Don't shrug," Thom said. "Everyone's getting theirs—why not me?"

"Indeed," I said, but I didn't know what that meant. I was just temporizing. I was thinking about Joe on the number five and wishing I were with him.

"I had to bring Owen down here," Thom said. "Stacey is in their apartment rehearsing with this other actor for the movie and probably making out." He looked at me and saw that did not rouse me. "You ready for this? In my apartment Gwennie and your son are doing the same."

This is not my life, it's drama. I just came back from my life. Let them make some sense of it. I don't have to.

"It's just like Chekov," Thom continued when I did not respond. "That's what I told her this morning when she called and asked me to fill her in on Chekov. Don't look surprised—I know a thing or two, Dad."

He looked around, lifted his behind off the bench when he saw Owen appeared to be started down the path, but sat back when Owen returned to the fence. "Say something to me," he said.

"How is it like Chekov?" I finally said.

"Actually not like *Three Sisters*, but God, a lot like *The Sea Gull*." There was someone at the end of our bench—an old lady startled into attention, like a bird on a branch just before it flies away from danger—but Thom didn't care. He got hold of one of my hands, and explained, "Everyone is in love with someone who doesn't love back."

Thom had to get up and settle an incipient fracas between Owen and a little girl who had joined him and his friend. I looked at the old lady and nodded and smiled a little.

"Nice day," she said, and then nodded and smiled back. She had no agenda, again as the kids say, and took up her magazine and left me to myself.

When Thom returned, I said, "Don't worry about all those things. It's merely drama."

Thom straightened and held himself still a moment, alert like the old lady and the bird. "You're right," he said. "It doesn't really have to do with me either. Why don't I come over later and give you a good rubdown—it's one of my many trades. And then, who knows, maybe."

I shook my head. I said, "No, that's drama, too. If they settle the baseball strike this week, you can come over for the first Mets game and we can talk about Chekov and the good old days when Keith Hernández played first."

Thom moved his head slowly from side to side. He said, "God, you're wise."

I guess this is as good a place as any to stop. Ha-ha.